The Prairie Dog Conspiracy

Books by Eric Wilson

The Tom and Liz Austen Mysteries

Also available by Eric Wilson

The Prairie Dog Conspiracy

A Tom Austen Mystery

by

ERIC WILSON

HarperCollins_PublishersLtd_

The author would like to thank The Vintage Locomotive Society for information on the Prairie Dog Central.

As in his other mysteries, Eric Wilson writes here about imaginary people in a real landscape.

Find Eric Wilson at www.ericwilson.com

http://www. harpercollins.com

First published in hardcover by HarperCollins Publishers Ltd: 1992
First published in paperback by HarperCollins Publishers Ltd: 1993
    Fourth printing: 1995
Revised paperback edition published by HarperCollins Publishers Ltd: 1996
    Third printing: 1999

Canadian Cataloguing in Publication Data

Wilson, Eric
  The prairie dog conspiracy

(A Tom Austen mystery)
ISBN 0-00-648177-9

I. Title.   II. Series: Wilson, Eric. A Tom Austen mystery.

PS8595.I583P7 1996   jC813'.54   C95-933353-3
PZ7.W55Pr 1996

99 00 01 02 ❖ OPM 10 9 8 7 6 5 4 3

Printed and bound in the United States

cover design: Richard Bingham
cover and chapter illustrations: Richard Row
logo photograph: Lawrence McLagan

This book is dedicated to my friends.
Your caring sustains me.

1

Tom Austen and his young cousin, Duncan Joy, were sitting in front of a fake fireplace in Duncan's basement detective office. With the case of the Ice Diamond wrapped up, things were getting back to normal in Petty Harbour.

"After you leave, Tom, things are going to be pretty quiet here," Duncan sighed. "I don't think another case will happen, and I'll never get the chance to be a famous detective!"

Both cousins were redheads. Duncan was ten, and Tom, fourteen. Tom's blue eyes studied the mystery novels on the bookshelf, travelled to a poster of Sherlock Holmes, then looked out at the narrow, winding streets of the Newfoundland fishing village where

Duncan lived.

At last he looked back at his cousin. "I used to think I'd never have a real mystery to solve. I called in tips to the police, I read every mystery novel I could lay my hands on—and still, nothing." Tom pulled his chair closer to Duncan's. "Then one day, it happened. I stumbled on something very peculiar, right in my home town of Winnipeg." Tom lowered his voice. "It was a particularly long, cold winter . . ."

Across from him, Duncan's eyes glowed with excitement.

* * *

The raid on the mystery house began at exactly 8:13 P.M. In charge of operations was Tom Austen, an eleven-year-old redhead soon to become a famous detective. For now, however, he was only known for his many freckles and friendly smile.

Beside Tom was Dietmar Oban, whose name was pronounced Deet-mar. He had brown hair and eyes, and always wore the latest styles. Dietmar's smile was usually self-confident, but this evening he looked plain scared.

"You're crazy, Austen," Dietmar whispered. "I'm not going inside that creepy place."

Tom didn't reply. He was studying the abandoned house with its blank windows and peeling paint. Icicles hung like crystal teeth from the roof, and a cold moon looked down from the black night. The yard was deep with snow.

"Did you hear me, Austen? I'm going home."

Tom looked at him. "What about the poems I've been writing for you to give Charity? You wouldn't want her to know who really wrote them, would you?"

"I admit your romantic words have been a hit with Charity," Dietmar said, staring at the abandoned house, "but I'm not so sure they're worth going in that place."

"I've written a new poem," Tom said. "It's yours, the minute we complete tonight's investigation of the mystery house."

"What's so important about this deserted place, Austen?"

"See that attic window? Last night there was a light up there, I'm sure of it."

"So tell the cops."

Tom shook his head. "I've already phoned in too many tips that didn't work out. My reputation is lower than a snake's belly. I've got to solve the mystery of this house without calling 911. So we're going inside ourselves. Nothing will happen. Don't be scared, Dietmar."

"I still want to go home."

"Relax—soon you'll be parked in front of your TV again. For now, enjoy the adventure."

"I don't like this," Dietmar muttered. "Not one little bit."

The boys began to break trail across the yard's icy crust. The wind twirled snow-devils into their faces.

"Look," Tom said, pointing. Another trail led across the snow from the lane behind the house. "This trail is recent," Tom said, kneeling to examine it. "There's a bit of snow drifted into the footprints, so they were probably made last night." He turned to Dietmar with triumphant eyes. "And last night was when I saw the light in the attic."

"Big deal," Dietmar muttered.

The boys followed the trail. The house had been empty now for a year. The porch roof sagged under a weight of snow, and the living-room window was cracked. The trail ended at a basement window.

"It's broken," Tom said. "I bet someone smashed it to get into the house." He looked at Dietmar. "My new poem's the best yet—Charity will worship you. So don't forget to follow me."

Tom landed in the basement with a soft thump. The air smelled of mold and rotting newspapers. His flashlight beam travelled over a broken sofa and some old cartons, then found wooden stairs.

Dietmar landed with a crash. "Ouch! I just sprained my ankle." He hobbled in a circle, testing it. "I'll wait here for you, Austen."

Tom grabbed his arm. "You're a rotten actor, Oban. Now follow me, and keep quiet."

"I don't like this!"

Slowly the boys tiptoed up the creaking stairs. A door at the top opened with a rusty squeal, then there was a sudden scrambling sound. As Dietmar yelped with fear, Tom swung his flashlight toward the kitchen counter, where a little brown mouse dashed into hiding.

Tom's mouth was dry and his heart thundered in his chest. The flashlight beam jiggled in his nervous hand as he and Dietmar entered the hallway. The rooms were completely empty. As they climbed the stairs to the second floor, every sound echoed between the bare walls.

In the upper hallway, they found empty bedrooms and more stairs. These were narrow, and the attic waited at the top. Dietmar's breathing was rough. Maintaining a tight grip on his arm, Tom gestured with the flashlight.

"We're going up to the attic," he whispered. "I'll make a few notes, then we're out of here. No problem."

Dietmar said nothing. His eyes bulged with fear, and he was gasping for air.

The attic stairs were covered with dust. Tom rubbed his nose, afraid of sneezing. The stairs creaked as the boys climbed to the top and opened the door.

The attic was a single bare room with a sloped ceiling. On the far wall was a closet, empty except for three wire hangers. Tom kneeled in the doorway and swept the flashlight beam across the floor.

"See how the dust has been disturbed? Someone's been up here recently."

"So what? Let's get out of this place!"

"In a minute." Still kneeling at the door, Tom wrote in his pocket notebook, then looked at the bare walls. "This could be a meeting place for some kind of gang. It's perfect for criminals."

"I'm going home," Dietmar said.

"Okay, I just want to . . ."

Tom's eyes grew huge. From somewhere downstairs came the squeal of rusty hinges.

* * *

Tom and Dietmar stared at each other, then desperately scrambled down the stairs. They could clearly hear footsteps and the sound of hinges as doors were opened and closed somewhere below.

"You idiot," Dietmar hissed at Tom. "We're doomed!"

Tom flashed his light from room to room, searching for an escape route. Outside one window was the porch roof, heavy with snow. "We can slide down the roof, and drop to the yard." With record speed, he pulled Dietmar to the window, and opened it. The cold wind blew into their faces.

"You first, Oban. I'll protect you."

"Why me? Isn't this roof safe?"

"Of course it is! Now hurry up!"

Crawling out the window, Dietmar stepped onto the roof above the porch. But the snow had a layer of slick ice on it, and Dietmar lost his balance. He flew through the air, and with a cry, plunged into the deep snow. Moments later he struggled free, and ran down the street.

Attracted by the noise, someone was rapidly climbing the stairs. Moving swiftly, Tom crossed the room and hid inside a closet.

A flashlight beam travelled around the room, then a man stepped inside. He was short and wore a parka. Tom saw the man limp as he walked to the window.

"Some crazy kid sneaking around here," the man muttered to himself, slamming the window shut.

The flashlight beam travelled around the walls. Tom shrank back behind the closet door. He listened to the man grumbling to himself as he left the room. On the stairs, the limp gave his footsteps a distinctive sound. When the man reached the attic, Tom stepped out of hiding. Keeping his eyes on the ceiling, he tiptoed into the hallway. The floor of the attic creaked as the man walked around. Tom wondered what was going on. One thing he knew for sure—he would soon return to the mystery house.

2

Later that night, Tom was in his detective office in the attic of his home. On one wall, he had put up a large map of Canada. Nearby, a poster displayed the grim faces of the nation's Most Wanted Criminals. Every day Tom memorized their scars and tattoos and shifty eyes, knowing that eventually he'd spot one of these desperados on the street. Then there would be an arrest, and he would be famous.

An old lamp glowed over the wooden desk where he worked on a computer file named *Mystery House*. He completed his notes on the man with the limp, then picked up the phone and called to see if Dietmar was okay. He got the family's answering machine, so he left a message.

Finished with the *Mystery House* file, Tom opened

another file named *fan letter* and continued working on his letter to Franklin W. Dixon, about the Hardy Boys. Tom was interested in learning how the author had made *The Twisted Claw* seem so real. Closing the file, Tom swivelled his chair to study a poster of Agatha Christie. She looked like a kindly grandmother, yet her brilliant mind had created a multitude of criminals and cheaters with schemes evil enough to keep some of the greatest detectives constantly busy.

His sister, Liz, called from downstairs. "Uncle Henry's making popcorn, Tom. Come join us!"

"Be right there," Tom replied.

Liz was an okay sister. Together, they were having some fun with their uncle, who was in charge while Mr. and Mrs. Austen were celebrating their anniversary with a trip to some remote areas of Mexico. Taking a final look at Canada's Most Wanted, Tom left the office and locked the door. As a precaution, he slipped a tiny piece of paper between the door and the frame. If the door was secretly opened, he'd find the paper on the floor and know that someone had been snooping.

Uncle Henry was in the kitchen, wearing a butter-stained apron and a chef's hat, old-fashioned spectacles and outdated clothes. "I wish your parents would get back," Uncle Henry said, pouring hot popcorn into bowls. It was delicious. "You arrived home late again tonight, Tom. You two are causing me a lot of worry. Liz, don't smile with your mouth full."

Liz was thirteen. She read a lot of books, and was superstitious. So far, detective work didn't interest her. She preferred horseback riding and swimming.

"We got a postcard from Mom and Dad," Liz told her brother. "They're having a great time in Mexico."

"Never travel," Uncle Henry warned them. "Every trip I take, something goes wrong."

"But then we'll never meet anyone," Tom said. "We won't find out about things."

"I know some interesting folks," Uncle Henry protested. "I told you about Sir Nigel, my cousin who owns the castle in Toronto. I'm also friends with the Maestro, that crackpot relative of your chum Dietmar Oban. I've had some good laughs with the Maestro!"

At that moment, Uncle Henry knocked over the salt. Liz sprang forward to toss a pinch over her left shoulder. "Do the same," she warned the others. "Otherwise, there'll be trouble for someone in this house."

Uncle Henry quickly did as instructed, but Tom shook his head. "I don't agree with that superstition. Throwing salt over your shoulder doesn't make sense."

"Just do it," Liz urged him.

"Nope," Tom said, shaking his head. "I don't see trouble coming up for me."

"You're making a mistake," Liz warned.

But Tom just smiled. He didn't believe in superstitions.

* * *

The walk to school in February was especially cold when the wind blew off the frozen prairie. The sun had not yet risen, so Tom burrowed deep into his winter clothes. At Queenston School, he collected a crossing-patrol vest and flag, then continued to the corner of

Kingsway and Waterloo. Earlier in the year, he had patrolled the busiest corner beside Queenston School. But after Tom had played some practical jokes, the principal punished him by appointing him to a corner that few kids used.

Tom tried some skids on the snowy sidewalk, then waited for something to do. A pale light was creeping into the sky, outlining the bare branches of trees and the shapes of houses. In the distance, kids crossed busy corners on their way to school, but nobody came Tom's way.

At last, he saw Dianne Dorchester approaching. She was the one reason Tom didn't mind this corner all that much. She wore a beautiful parka and expensive mitts that had been made in the Arctic.

"Hi, Tom," she said, stopping at his corner. "Busy this morning?"

Tom cast down his eyes, feeling a blush spread across his face. Dianne was so pretty he could never think of anything to say. "Business is okay, thanks," he murmured.

"Guess what, Tom? My father was on TV last night talking about his company."

Tom nodded. "I saw the interview. It was interesting how he defended Dorchester Industries' record on the environment. He had quite an argument with that woman from Save Our Earth."

"Those environmentalists say our mill in White River is causing damage to the water, but Daddy says it isn't true. I wish they would leave us alone."

Tom glanced down Waterloo Street. A pickup truck was coming their way, moving slowly. It was a late model Ford, its black paint showing rust. There was a small camper mounted on the back.

"Better wait to cross," Tom cautioned Dianne.

As the pickup came closer, the driver stared at Dianne. His hair was a dark red, and a cigarette dangled from his thin lips. Stopping at the corner, the driver rolled down his window. "Hey, you," he called to Tom. "Where's Queenston School?"

"Straight down Kingsway," Tom replied, pointing. "You can't miss it."

"Thanks, kid." The driver looked at Dianne again, then put the pickup into gear and drove away.

Tom watched it go. "There's mud obscuring his license plate. Maybe that's deliberate. Notice, too, that Rex isn't going toward the school, even though he asked how to find it."

"Who's Rex?" Dianne asked.

"The driver of that pickup."

"How do you know his name?"

"I saw it on a little badge sewed to his parka."

Dianne smiled. "Tom, you've really got a mind for detective work. Why are you so into it?"

"It's like a jigsaw, I guess. The detective has to put the pieces together. Do you know what a cryptogram is?"

Dianne shook her head.

"It's a code that spies use to disguise a message. It looks like a bunch of numbers, but secretly they represent letters. I'm becoming an expert on cryptograms, in case I ever need to decode one."

Dianne's blue eyes studied him. "Sometimes, Tom, you're *so* strange."

He blushed.

"Do you think you'll ever get a *real* case to solve?"

"I sure hope so," Tom replied, eagerly.

"Well, see you around, Tom." Dianne walked on toward school.

Tom sighed, gazing after her.

* * *

His patrol duties over, Tom walked to Queenston School. The hallway was full of kids laughing and talking. With them was the school's new mascot, a collie known as Lassie. Tom knelt beside the dog for a hug, then saw the school custodian approaching.

"Hi, Walt," Tom said. "It's a cold day."

"You bet. Busy on patrol?"

"Not too bad, thanks."

Walt Kennedy was a big man with friendly eyes and not much hair. Getting Lassie for the school was his suggestion, and he'd fought for the idea when the principal didn't agree. As Tom spoke to Walt, they were joined by his daughter, Charity, a friendly girl with dark hair and eyes, and a sweet smile.

Walt said goodbye, and walked slowly away. "Poor Daddy," Charity said, watching him with sad eyes. "All he thinks about these days is money."

"Why's that? He's got a steady job."

"My little brother, Donald, is very sick. Daddy read about a new medicine that's only available in the U.S., but it costs a fortune."

"Maybe we could raise some money at school," Tom suggested. "Pizza sales, or something like that."

"That's a nice idea, Tom. Thank you. I'll tell Daddy you want to help."

Charity went into the office and Tom continued along the hallway, talking to kids and teachers. Upstairs, he was grabbed by Dietmar Oban. "Thanks for the free ride down the roof, Austen. I really needed that!"

"Hey, take it easy. I didn't know it was that icy."

"Where's my poem?"

Tom handed him a sheet of paper. "Charity will love this one. I kind of wish I'd saved it to give Dianne."

"Forget it, Austen. It's my payment for going into that creepy house." Dietmar glanced at the poem. "This reads okay." He studied Tom with suspicious eyes. "If you've got any more plans for raiding the mystery house, I . . . won't . . . be . . . there."

"Okay, but *I'm* going back."

"When?"

"Tonight."

"Why?"

"Because something strange is going on. I'm convinced that guy I saw is part of a gang, and the abandoned house is their headquarters. In *The Twisted Claw* the pirates have great headquarters."

Dietmar shook his head. "You're obsessed."

"Here's the strange thing, Dietmar: why would anybody enter that abandoned house at all? I heard that the bank owns it and they're planning to tear it down."

"Your father's in the police force. Tell him."

"I will, as soon as he and Mom get back from Mexico."

"Well, Austen, in my opinion . . ."

Dietmar suddenly stopped speaking. Charity was walking by.

"Hi, Charity," Dietmar said. "Can I talk to you for a minute?" He glared at Tom. "Alone."

Tom smiled. "See you guys in class."

Dietmar slipped the envelope containing Tom's poem into Charity's hand. Blushing, she quickly thanked him and hurried into the classroom. Dietmar, following right behind, bumped into the doorway.

Red hearts were hung everywhere in anticipation of February 14, which was fast approaching. A large box, decorated with crepe paper and hearts, accepted Valentines for others in the class. Passing the box, Tom slipped in two envelopes. One was for Charity, the other for Dianne. They were both nice—Tom was great friends with Charity, but his heart belonged to Dianne.

He walked up the aisle, his eyes on Dianne's golden hair. She was leaning over a Valentine card, making it by hand. Tom wondered which lucky person would receive the card. His heart fluttered briefly with hope as he took his seat in front of her and opened *The Twisted Claw*.

Dianne tapped him on the shoulder. "May I borrow your ruler, Tom?"

Tom turned to face Dianne. His hands shook slightly as he gave her the ruler. She smiled at him with eyes that were the colour of the sea. His face flamed, and he quickly returned to his book.

At the end of reading time, their teacher, Mr. Price, stood up at his desk. He had sandy-coloured hair, green eyes and a friendly smile. Every week, he wore something new, and today it was a suede belt patterned with whirling colours.

Mr. Price sat on the edge of his desk. There were tassels on the leather shoes at the end of his long legs. "I saw your father on TV last night, Dianne. Doesn't your mother usually speak for the company?"

"She's not been well, Mr. Price. All the demonstrations by Save Our Earth are wearing her down. She doesn't even like going downtown anymore because of the demonstrations outside our office tower."

"That's a shame," Mr. Price said. He looked around the room. "So, who's got something to share with us today?"

Dianne held up her hand. "Tom told me that he's a detective." She giggled. "I think he should tell the class about it."

"Good idea," Mr. Price said. "Go for it, Tom."

Slowly Tom stood up, face burning with embarrassment. Everyone was watching him, except Dietmar, who yawned and tried to look bored. "Well," Tom said quietly, "I like reading detective stories, and I'm kind of hoping for a case of my own soon. I wouldn't mind being a famous gumshoe some day—that means a private eye."

"Gumshoe," Dietmar snorted. "I wonder what's stuck to the bottom? I'd hate to know."

Dianne was smiling. "Tell them about the cryptograms."

Briefly, Tom explained the secret codes. "Spies also use disappearing ink."

"What's the point of that?" Dietmar asked. "They wouldn't be able to read anything."

"By slowly warming the paper over a candle," Tom replied, "the message is revealed."

"Unless the paper goes up in smoke."

Ignoring Dietmar, Tom picked up a book about cryptograms. "This contains some interesting codes. It's in my desk, if anyone would like to read it."

"Boring," Dietmar said with another big yawn, but Charity smiled at Tom. "I'll read it," she said. "It sounds interesting."

Tom sat down. Once again, he had impressed the wrong girl. Anyway, he would show them all that he really was a detective. He thought of the mystery house, deciding right then and there that he would return that evening.

3

Alone in the mystery house, Tom shivered.

Was it fear, or the cold? The empty house, bare of furniture and carpets, chilled him. His breath was white in the flashlight beam as he climbed the attic stairs. He was afraid of what lay ahead, but he wanted to find out what was really going on in this house.

The wooden stairs creaked under his feet. Ahead was the attic door. Reaching out, Tom pushed it open. Sweeping his flashlight across the room, he saw the closet with the three bare hangers.

Tom studied the attic and made notes. Suddenly, his hair stood on end. From below came a rusty squeal of hinges, followed by the murmur of voices. They were coming closer! Quickly he looked for a place to hide— his only hope was the closet.

Safely inside, he squeezed against the wall and clicked off his flashlight—just in time. Tom saw two men enter the attic. One was tall, and both were disguised in ski masks. The shorter one was the man with the limp!

Switching off their flashlights, the men stood together in the moonlight that was coming through a small window.

"Leave your ski mask on," the shorter one said. "Some kid was here last night, snooping around. He might return—I don't want anyone seeing our faces." He limped over to the window and peered out. "We're covered for the ceremony," he continued. "It's next Monday at 4 P.M. You're certain you'll be there?"

"Yeah," the other man growled. "No problem."

Their voices were low, muffled by the fabric of the ski masks. Tom's heart thumped as he watched them.

"My girlfriend will be working with us again. I'm calling this Operation Golden Child. Any problems with that name?"

"Nope."

"Your instructions are inside this envelope. After you've memorized the plans, destroy them."

"There's one thing I don't like." The tall man's voice seemed familiar to Tom, but it was only a low murmur. He listened hard as the man continued speaking. "Is the death necessary?"

"Of course. It's the only way."

"But . . ."

"Operation Golden Child will make us a fortune. Don't weasel out now. Remember, I can still pin the last job on you." The man glanced around the attic.

Tom pressed harder against the wall, hardly breathing. "We'll meet again tomorrow."

"Here?"

"No, it's too risky. That kid who was snooping around may be back."

Their voices faded down the stairs. Tom leaned against the wall, hardly daring to breathe, memorizing everything he'd heard so he could enter it in his computer file. He could hardly believe it, but it had happened at last.

He'd stumbled on a major crime.

* * *

Back at home, Tom sat in front of the fireplace with Liz and Uncle Henry. They were chomping popcorn and enjoying the flames while Tom described his experience in the mystery house.

"So," he said in conclusion, "obviously those guys are planning a heist."

Uncle Henry's brow furrowed. "Where'd you pick up that word?"

"From a detective story," Tom replied. "Heist is criminal slang. It means a major robbery. For example, hijacking gold bullion from an armored car."

"So," Liz asked, "what are those guys planning to rob?"

"Next Monday at 4 P.M., a ceremony will be held at the Legislative Building, where the provincial government meets." Tom showed them a newspaper picture. "Our province is receiving this statue, a replica of the Golden Boy. It's a gift from the same place in France where the original statue was made—and the perfect target for a heist. It all makes sense."

"Recently," Uncle Henry said, "I wrote a history article about the Golden Boy. Everyone has seen him, standing high above the city on top of the Legislative Building, but few people know his history."

"He was created by Charles Gaudet," Liz said, "the same guy who did the bronze buffaloes inside the building."

"Very good!"

"The statue is four meters high," Tom added. "That's more than 13 feet, which is pretty tall for a boy. He holds a sheaf of wheat, symbolizing Manitoba's agriculture, and the torch of progress."

"I was wrong," Uncle Henry smiled. "You know all about the Golden Boy."

"I just did an essay about him for school," Liz explained. "Tom helped with the research."

"The statue is sheathed in 23.5 karat gold," Tom said. He pointed at the newspaper picture. "This replica of the statue stands more than a meter tall, and is also made with gold. It's a nice gift, and worth a fortune."

"How can those guys steal it?" Liz said. "Won't there be heavy security?"

"I'm not sure about the security," Tom replied, "but these men have a secret plan. Obviously, Golden Child is their code name for the gift statue. They'll probably steal the statue during the ceremony, then demand a ransom in the millions." He slapped his notebook. "I've recorded my theory in here. I know I'm right."

"So," Uncle Henry said, "you're going to call the police?"

Tom looked into the flames. "Well, I'm not *that* sure. I've called them before with some theories, but nothing has ever worked out. Maybe I'd better assemble a bit more information."

* * *

After school a few days later, Tom stood alone on patrol as a winter storm took over the city. Big flakes settled on nearby houses and trees as he waited for kids to pass the corner of Kingsway and Waterloo.

Who were the two men in the attic? Was Golden Child really a code name for the gift from France? What would happen at the presentation of the statue? Would it be stolen?

As the questions whirled around inside Tom's head, he saw Dianne Dorchester coming his way. Soft flakes drifted down around her face and settled on her beautiful parka.

"Hi, Tom," she smiled.

Blushing, he quietly replied, "Hi," and fingered a special Valentine's poem he had in his pocket for Dianne. Tom wondered if this was the right moment to give it to her.

"Thanks for helping with my homework before school." Dianne yawned. "Last night, my parents came back from shopping with some new videos, and I watched my favourite movie twice. Then I fell asleep over my assignment!"

"I have to finish my homework first. It's a rule at our house."

Dianne smiled. "Maybe I'll invite you over to my house sometime to watch a movie. We've got shelves and shelves of videos to choose from."

"I'd like to visit your house," Tom said shyly. "It looks beautiful from the outside. I've also heard that you have an excellent security system—maybe I could test it, to be sure it works properly."

"It was installed by professionals," Dianne replied. "Well, see you tomorrow, Tom."

As he watched Dianne's parka disappear into the storm, Tom looked at his watch, then decided to follow her—this was the perfect opportunity to give her the poem. He knew that five minutes of patrol duty still remained, but Dianne was usually the last person he saw. Besides, maybe she'd be so touched, she would invite him to the Dorchester home today and he could watch videos with her.

As he hurried along the street, Tom heard wheels crunching along the snowy street. Turning, he saw a pickup truck approaching. At the wheel was the man named Rex, talking on a cellular phone. As Rex drove past, he looked at Tom with beady eyes.

At Academy Road, Rex turned right and disappeared among the many vehicles that used the busy street. Tom could see Dianne on the far corner, looking in the window of an art gallery. Above his head, a traffic light stayed red for what seemed a very long time. Buses and cars churned past as Tom impatiently waited.

Finally, Tom got across Academy Road, but Dianne had disappeared down Waterloo Street. He hurried past the houses, his feet slipping on the sidewalk. The snow was starting to collect on his head and shoulders.

Once again, the pickup came out of the blanket of falling snow, moving south on Waterloo. Rex was talking so intensely on the cellular phone that he didn't even notice Tom as he passed him by.

Tom turned onto Wellington Crescent, a street of expensive houses and estates that curved along the Assiniboine River. Dianne lived some distance away, near the end of Wellington, but there was no sign of her now as Tom looked down the snowy street. A brown van slowly passed Tom, moving east. He didn't give it much notice, until something started his heart pounding. The van had an aerial for a cellular phone!

Tom started running. Something was wrong; he had to find Dianne and warn her that Rex might be monitoring her movements, using his cellular phone. He saw her alone in the distance, trudging home. The van slowed down, then it pulled up beside her.

Dianne smiled at the person inside. "Hi there," she said, her faint words drifting to Tom through the snow. "A ride would be great, thanks."

"No," Tom cried. "Don't get in that van!"

Hearing him, Dianne turned. "Tom?" Her voice was muffled across the snowy distance. "What's wrong?"

Beside her, the van door opened. A hand reached out toward Dianne.

"Watch out!" Tom yelled. "Dianne . . . No . . . !"

It was too late. The hand seized Dianne, and pulled her into the van. There was a faint scream, then the door slammed and within seconds the van was gone. Dianne Dorchester had been kidnapped.

* * *

Within minutes, Wellington Crescent was no longer quiet. Sirens screamed. Police cars arrived and skidded to a stop. Officers jumped out. Red and blue lights swept the snow and the trees, shining on the spectators who gathered in the driveways of nearby houses.

As soon as the van had disappeared with Dianne inside, Tom had run to the Dorchester Estate and alerted a guard. Now several security guards stood beside him, providing protection as he waited to speak to the police. The sky was dark, and snow continued to fall. Tom's heart thumped in his chest whenever he thought about Dianne being pulled into the van. If that traffic light hadn't delayed him, she might be safe now.

Another police car arrived on the scene. Out stepped Officer Leonard Rice along with Inspector Rachel Elberg. Both served with his Dad on the Winnipeg City Police and were friends of his parents. "Are you okay?" they asked, approaching Tom. He nodded.

"So," Inspector Elberg said, "you've already talked to our police officers—anything to add?"

Tom shook his head. "Any luck with the roadblocks?"

"No," the Inspector replied. Her eyes studied the scene as she spoke to Tom. "But we've located the van, abandoned on a side street. It had been stolen. A neighbour saw another van driving away—it's likely Dianne was taken away inside."

"You're hearing secret police information," Officer Rice cautioned Tom. "Don't tell anyone about the second van."

He nodded. "What about Rex, the driver of the pickup?"

"We've issued an APB, but so far nothing. He may already be in hiding."

Inspector Elberg looked at Tom. "I've sent a message to Mexico to get your parents home fast—your Dad will lead the kidnapping investigation. Unfortunately, they're trekking in remote mountains, so it may take some time until I can reach them."

A truck came out of the night, moving fast. It was painted with the swirling logo of a local TV station, and had aerials on the roof for transmitting live broadcasts. As the truck screeched to a stop, a reporter and his camera crew tumbled out and ran toward Tom.

"Were you kidnapped, too?" the reporter demanded.

Tom shielded his eyes as a powerful light was switched on. "No, but I saw it happen. My name's Tom Austen, and . . ."

"Wait a minute," the reporter interrupted. "We're not getting sound." He turned toward the truck and yelled, "What's the problem, Jenny?"

"Don't get rattled," a voice replied from inside. "We had a little problem, but the sound's okay now. Go for it, Bryan."

The light on the camera swung to the reporter. "I'm Bryan Newgass, reporting live from the scene of a terrible crime. Moments ago Dianne Dorchester, daughter of the President of Dorchester Industries, was kidnapped from this street in an exclusive Winnipeg neighbourhood. With me is the only witness to the event, young Tom Austen." The light blazed in Tom's eyes. "How did it all happen, Tom? Tell us what you saw."

Tom described everything that had happened. When

he was finished, Bryan Newgass said, "Do you want to be a detective, Tom, and become famous?"

"Sure!" Tom's eyes glowed. "That would be great."

"Do you have any theories about Dianne's kidnapping, Tom? Who did it? What would Sherlock Holmes do now? This is your big chance."

Tom blushed. He could see a smirk on the reporter's face. "I . . ."

Bryan Newgass turned to the camera. "Perhaps it's time for our young detective to turn matters over to the police. Thanks for talking to us, Tom . . . Now we'll talk to . . ."

Tom grabbed the reporter's arm. "You're not being fair!"

Bryan Newgass stared at him. "What?"

"I've already got a theory. I'll start investigating tomorrow, and I'll find Dianne!"

"Well, then, what's your theory?"

Tom hesitated. "Well . . . I . . . maybe I shouldn't say."

The man laughed.

"All right," Tom said. "I'll tell you." He was angry now. "I first got suspicious when a man in a pickup truck asked directions to my school, then didn't go there. He had the name 'Rex' on his jacket. I think Rex made up that question so he could slow down and study Dianne. That way he'd recognize her again."

"Okay so far," Bryan Newgass said.

"I also believe that Dianne knew someone in the van, otherwise she would never have accepted a ride. It could even be someone from our school."

"Very interesting." Bryan Newgass gazed at Tom briefly, then quickly turned to face the camera. "I'm

Brian Newgass, live at the scene. Next we will talk to the police, but first, this."

The camera beam died. "Time for a commercial." Bryan Newgass slapped Tom's back with a big hand. "Thanks for the interview. It's great talking to a genuine boy detective!"

Tom didn't comment. He just turned and walked away. Bryan Newgass had made him feel like a fool.

* * *

The next day at school, Tom was a celebrity. Kids crowded around him in the hallway, staring, and several teachers stopped for a chat. One was a tense young woman named Ms. Ashmeade. "I'm very angry with that reporter, Bryan Newgass," she said. "I thought you were doing very well, Tom, until he cut you off."

"I agree completely." This came from Mr. Stones, a shy teacher who wore a button reading NO NEUTRON BOMBS. "You handled the interview well, Tom. Congratulations."

"Thanks, sir."

Mr. Price joined the group. "Talking about the kidnapping?" His green eyes settled on Tom. "The TV station repeated your interview with Bryan Newgass on the late news. You looked good."

Ms. Ashmeade nodded. "Very self-assured."

"Tom told my class about his interest in detective work," Mr. Price said, looking at the other teachers. "He really seems to have a knack for it."

"Yes, I know," Mr. Stones said. He rattled some coins in his pocket. "I'm a member of the Sherlock

Holmes Society, so I've often discussed the great one's cases with Tom."

"Your father's with the police," Ms. Ashmeade said to Tom. "What's wrong with them? How'd the kidnappers get away so easily? They had your description of the van, so why didn't they find it? In my opinion, they bungled."

"That's not fair," Tom protested. "Besides, the police did find the van. There wasn't any bungling!"

Mr. Stones looked surprised. "The van was found? But how did the kidnappers escape with Dianne?"

"In a second vehicle," Tom said. Then he blushed red. Like a fool, he'd given away a police secret. "Pretend I never said anything, okay? Only the police know that secret."

A tall man suddenly appeared beside Tom. "What secret?"

Tom looked up at Mr. Nicholson, the principal of Queenston School. He wore a grey three-piece suit and had a small grey moustache. His hair was grey and thinning, and he wore rimless spectacles.

"It's not important, sir," Tom replied. "Just something about the kidnapping."

"I think as principal of this school, I should know what's going on."

"I'm not supposed to tell, sir."

Mr. Nicholson stared down at Tom. He was very tall. Then he turned to the teachers. "No more gossiping. You're late for class."

As Ms. Ashmeade went into her classroom, Mr. Price turned to Mr. Stones. "Is your class still taking a special trip next week, John?"

"Yes, and the principal is joining us," Mr. Stones

replied. "We're riding the *Prairie Dog Central* to the north. It's a special trip to celebrate the Manitoba Railway Pioneers. I'm a member because my parents both worked on trains."

"I'd love my class to go along. Any chance?"

"Well, I'm not sure . . ."

"It's really important," Mr. Price said. "Dianne's classmates will be upset about her kidnapping. This trip would help take their minds off it."

"You're right," Mr. Stones replied. "I'll organize something. Perhaps they could add an extra passenger car." He turned to Tom. "Ever been aboard the *Prairie Dog*?"

"Just once," Tom replied, "when I was small. I still remember the old-fashioned steam engine."

"Can't you just picture Sherlock Holmes on that train?"

"You bet!"

Mr. Stones said goodbye. Tom smiled at Mr. Price as they walked toward their classroom. "That trip sounds fun, sir."

"I think so too, Tom. By the way, I wonder if you'd tell the class about your experience yesterday?"

"Sure."

"Nothing about the second van, of course. As you mentioned, it's a police secret."

As they entered the classroom, Mr. Price looked at the quiet students. "This is a sad Valentine's Day for all of us, but I believe Dianne will come home safely."

Janet Symon raised her hand. "When she does, could we have another Valentine's Day?"

"Good idea," the teacher replied.

Grant Peterson raised his hand. "Sir, did Dianne make a mistake?"

"Kids are talking about it," his brother David added. "She walked right up to the van, and was about to get inside when she was grabbed. You told us never to ride with strangers."

"You're right," Mr. Price replied, "so she must have known and trusted the driver. Isn't that your feeling, Tom?"

Slowly, Tom stood up. "Yes, I think she knew the driver of the van."

"Tell us what happened."

Tom looked straight ahead, avoiding the sight of Dianne's empty desk. Only yesterday she'd sat there, making Valentine's cards. He carefully told his story again. "Do you really think she'll come back safely, sir?"

Mr. Price nodded. "As soon as the kidnappers get their ransom, you'll see her again. It'll be an upsetting experience for Dianne, of course, but she's a self-confident girl. She should be fine." He looked around at the sad faces. "Let's review our Signposts for Safety."

Flo Connolly raised her hand. "Always use the same route between school and home. Know where the block parents live."

"Don't let anyone get close enough to grab you," Brett Blackwood suggested.

"Run if you have to," Patrick Lundrigan added, "or scream."

"Scream good and loud," Dietmar Oban said. "Pretend you looked in the mirror, and saw Tom Austen's face. A living nightmare for sure."

"Funny, funny," Tom scowled.

"Let's get to work," Mr. Price said. "You'll recall that we learned library research skills last month. I now have an assignment for each of you."

"Homework," Dietmar groaned. "I hate it!"

Mr. Price smiled at him. "Your task is simple, Dietmar. Memorize the entire Dewey Decimal System and give me a full written report on how it works."

"*What*? That'll take hours of work, sir!"

Mr. Price grinned. "I'm only kidding, Dietmar." He looked around the room. "In honour of our resident detective, you'll be researching criminal cases."

"Thanks, Austen," Dietmar glowered.

"Research your topics at the Public Library," Mr. Price told his students. "Use the vertical file—it's brimming with information."

"What's my topic?" Tom asked. "Murder?"

Mr. Price consulted a list he held in his hand. "Check the information on drunk driving, Tom, and make a report on two of the court cases."

Knuckles hammered on the classroom door. "Message from the office," a girl said. "Tom Austen is wanted there, immediately." Her curious eyes stared at him. "I saw you on TV. You were good."

"Thanks!"

Downstairs, Tom found Officer Leonard Rice standing in the hallway with the principal, who wiggled his finger in Tom's face. "You're turning into a regular celebrity, Tom Austen. We've been swamped with calls all morning from the media. Can't get a stitch of work done around here."

Tom shrugged his shoulders, not knowing what to say to that. Mr. Nicholson was always complaining about something. Rumour had it he was trying to take early retirement.

"Busy with work, William?" Officer Rice asked.

Mr. Nicholson nodded. "My stomach's in terrible shape. I think I'm developing an ulcer from all the stress around here."

"Aren't you planning to retire soon?"

Mr. Nicholson looked annoyed. "I can't afford it at the moment."

"A few more years won't hurt," Officer Rice said, slapping him on the back.

Mr. Nicholson pulled back his cuff to look at a gold watch on his wrist. "I'm expecting an important phone call. You'll have to excuse me."

"Nice watch," Officer Rice said. "If you sold that, you could probably retire."

Mr. Nicholson nodded. "I thought buying it would cheer me up, but I was wrong. The thing cost a mint, and now my wife is suggesting that *she'd* like to be cheered up with a holiday in Florida."

As the principal went into his office, Walt Kennedy came their way with Lassie, who wagged her tail vigorously when she saw Tom. The custodian looked at Officer Rice. "I haven't seen you for a while, Leonard. Are you here about the kidnapping?"

"That's right, Walt, I'm just seeing how our young detective is making out." Officer Rice smiled. "Are you still playing basketball?"

Walt shook his big head. "I haven't played for some time."

"Well, it's good to see you again. I wondered what happened after . . ." Officer Rice suddenly turned to

Tom. "How are you doing, Tom? That was a pretty big scare yesterday. It's a shame your parents aren't here. I bet you could use them right about now."

"I'm all right, thanks. Any news about Dianne, Officer Rice?"

He shook his head. "That fellow Rex with the pickup truck has disappeared, and there's no trace of the second van."

"Isn't it a secret?" Tom asked.

"Not any more," Rice replied. "We're about to release a description of the second van to the media. We're hoping someone has spotted it."

"I'll be watching, too," Tom said. "I'm sure I can help find Dianne."

4

The next day, Tom burned with anger.

He was in the glass-walled tower at The Forks, Winnipeg's traditional meeting area. For 6,000 years, people have gathered where the Assiniboine River flows into the Red, but few were ever unhappier than Tom Austen.

Tom had arranged to meet Dietmar at The Forks and had waited for forty-five minutes. When Dietmar hadn't turned up, Tom tried to spot him from the observation tower. He looked at the two rivers, their icy surfaces white with snow. On the Red River, bearded men in toques were racing dog-sled teams, watched by cheering crowds. On the Assiniboine, teams were competing on snowshoes while other people created giant ice sculptures. It was all part of the *Festival du Voyageur*, recalling the history of the first Europeans to explore the west.

Looking down at the outdoor rink, Tom now understood why Dietmar had skipped their meeting. Two cheerful people were skating under the pale winter sky—Dietmar Oban and Charity Kennedy.

Tom stepped into the elevator, and rode down to give Dietmar a piece of his mind. Outside, the air was cold but pleasant. People were laughing together, little kids walked past with balloons, and everyone seemed happy. Especially Dietmar, who spotted Tom from the rink and waved innocently.

"Hi there," Dietmar exclaimed. "I got here early and saw Charity skating alone. Naturally, I wanted to keep her company."

"Naturally," Tom replied, "but you didn't have to ditch *me*!"

Charity skated over to join them. She wore a soft white toque, and her skin glowed. "Hi Tom, it's wonderful to see you."

"Thanks," he said, smiling. "You're a good skater, Charity. I saw you from the tower."

Dietmar laughed. "Were you up there watching for kidnappers, Austen?"

"No. I was looking for you, because you weren't where you were supposed to be."

"Come join us, Tom," Charity said.

"Thanks, but I haven't got enough money to rent skates."

Dietmar grinned. "Trainer skates are free."

"Okay, then," Charity said, "we can watch some festival events together." She turned to Dietmar. "Isn't it great that we've run into Tom?"

"Sure thing," Dietmar replied. "I'm thrilled."

* * *

Down by the river, they watched some races, then Charity took a picture of Tom and Dietmar beside an impressive snow sculpture. Dietmar suggested they do their own sculpture of the Golden Boy, and before long they'd completed a nice representation of the Winnipeg landmark.

"Not bad," Tom said, patting more snow under the boy's chin. "If we had some gold paint, we'd win the prize for Best Sculpture, for sure."

Charity smiled. "This is fun."

"Know what's happening on Monday?" Tom asked her. "The gift statue of the Golden Boy is being presented at the Legislative Building." Stepping closer to Charity he dropped his voice to a whisper. "I think some criminals may try to steal the gift. It's worth a fortune."

Dietmar grinned. "This guy does nothing but read mysteries and dream up crimes to solve. You'll never be a real detective, Austen, trust me on this."

"Oh yeah? I bet I'll find Dianne."

Charity touched his hand. "Oh, Tom, I wish you could."

"I'll do it," he replied.

Dietmar snorted. "Not a chance. She'll come home, but it won't be thanks to Queenston School's very own boy detective."

* * *

Shielding his eyes, Tom looked across the Red River at St. Boniface, the community which sponsored the festival. In 1818, the people of St. Boniface built a huge cathedral overlooking the river; 150 years later it burned, leaving only broken walls and a high facade topped by a stone cross.

A large crowd lined Avenue Taché in front of the cathedral. The people were cheering dog sleds as they crossed the finish line of their race. Tom watched a man leave the group and walk toward the cathedral.

"Hey," Tom exclaimed, "that guy is limping!"

"So what, Austen?"

Tom pulled Dietmar aside. "I never told you, Dietmar, but I went back to the mystery house without you. There were two men there, and one of them definitely had a limp. They're plotting a heist to steal the Golden Boy replica at the ceremony on Monday afternoon. That could be one of them, over at the cathedral. He's got the same build and he's even wearing a ski mask that looks the same!"

"What are you talking about, Austen? Now you've really gone crazy."

"I'm convinced I'm right this time! Their operation is code-named Golden Child. I heard them myself!"

"Then call 911 and get him arrested."

"No way, I need some proof." Tom grabbed Dietmar's arm. "Come on, let's go check him out."

"Forget it, Austen. You're in over your head."

Tom turned to Charity, who was still working on their snow sculpture. "I hear Dietmar's been giving you some poems, Charity."

She blushed. "Well, yes."

"Dietmar's a great poet, right? He's told you that, right?"

"Yes . . . Why, what's wrong?"

Dietmar put a hand over Tom's mouth. "Okay, I'll go with you."

Tom smiled at Charity. "Nothing's wrong, but Dietmar and I have something to do."

Charity nodded. "I'm staying right here. My Dad's worried about me getting kidnapped, so he's meeting me to ride home together. Want to come with us on the bus?"

"Sure," Tom said. "See you later."

Tom and a reluctant Dietmar crossed the river and climbed some wide stairs to Avenue Taché. There were a lot of people around, but Tom's suspect was nowhere in sight. "Rats," he exclaimed, scanning the scene. "We've lost him. I was too busy convincing you to come along. I should have been watching my suspect."

"Great," Dietmar said. "I'm getting cold, and I wouldn't mind something to eat. Let's go back to The Forks."

"There he is!"

A man had emerged from behind the cathedral, and now limped quickly along a frozen path that led past the grave of Louis Riel in the direction of Boulevard Provencher. He wore a maroon-coloured parka, and a ski mask completely covered his head.

"I've got a theory that explains why he was at the cathedral," Tom said. "Want to hear it?"

"Nope," Dietmar replied.

"He's finding a place to hide the gift statue, after it's stolen. Behind that cross would be perfect. Who'd look up there?"

"Great theory, Austen, but one question. How would he get a heavy gold statue up to the cross? Rent a crane?"

Tom's face fell. "You may have a point, or is that the top of your head?"

"Funny line, Austen, but I've heard it before."

"I'm not surprised." Tom looked at the distant figure of the man. "He's almost reached the boulevard. We'd better follow him."

"Forget it. I've had enough snow and cold for the day. I'm going back to find Charity."

"I'll go with you and we can discuss *my* poetry with Charity."

"You know what, Austen? You play rough."

Dietmar fell into step with Tom and they hurried along Avenue Taché to the boulevard, which was crowded with traffic. On the far side, they saw Tom's suspect, limping along Rue St. Joseph. "He's heading toward the railway," Tom said. "He's probably going to walk the tracks across the trestle to downtown Winnipeg."

Dietmar grinned. "Your brain must resemble Swiss cheese, Austen. Why didn't he cross on the Provencher Bridge? It's got a sidewalk."

"He's afraid of the police. Didn't you see their checkpoint at the west end of the bridge? They're watching for suspects in Dianne's kidnapping, but that guy's probably afraid of being remembered after he steals the statue."

Dietmar shook his head. "What an imagination! You should write mysteries."

"No way. The moment I graduate from high school, I'll be hanging out my shingle as a gumshoe."

Dietmar pointed at a man walking along Taché.

"There's Walt, on his way to meet Charity at The Forks. Maybe I should join him."

"Not a chance," Tom replied.

As the boys talked, they followed the suspect in the direction of the tracks. He paused once, looking at them, then continued on his way. In the yards of comfortable-looking houses, kids were building snowmen or creating angels; a woman called *Bonjour* to Tom and Dietmar as they passed. The scene was peaceful until a passing car backfired with a sound like a gunshot, making the suspect spin around. This time he stared directly at the boys.

"Oh no," Tom exclaimed. "He can tell we're following him." He gripped Dietmar's arm. "We'll move closer and see what happens. If he's a crook, he'll make a break for it."

"This is crazy," Dietmar protested as Tom dragged him along. "I was having fun skating with Charity. Now I'm a junior detective *and I hate it!*"

"You could end up on TV, Oban. Think about the fame!"

"Forget it. I don't want to be interviewed by Bryan Newgass. He made a fool of you, and he'd do the same to me."

"Look!" Tom pointed at the suspect. "Just like I predicted—he's making a break for it!"

The man was limping quickly along the tracks toward a railway trestle. Reaching it, he looked over his shoulder at the boys and then began to cross. Beside him on the westbound tracks, a huge freight train waited its turn to enter the railway yards. Below was the frozen Red River.

"He's crossing to downtown Winnipeg," Tom said. "We've lost him."

"Aren't you going to follow?" Dietmar asked.

"No way," Tom replied. "That trestle carries the CNR mainline traffic. Trains use it all the time." He started walking toward the trestle. "But let's get closer, and see where the suspect goes on the other side."

It was cold by the trestle. Below, on the frozen river, a dog team raced past, yelping with excitement as people shouted encouragement from the finish line. In the distance, the sun sparkled against the windows of the observation tower at The Forks.

"I resign as a detective," Dietmar said. "I'm frozen, and Charity is waiting for us. Forget your suspect, we've lost him."

"Maybe you're right, but . . ." Tom stared at Dietmar as he went out on the trestle. "Hey! What are you doing, Oban?"

"I'm taking another route back to The Forks."

"Get off those tracks, you idiot! There's a train coming—I heard it whistle a minute ago."

"Sure, Austen, I believe you." Dietmar walked further out on the trestle. Below him, another dog team headed for the finish line. "I'll race you back to The Forks—you better get moving."

"Come back, you idiot!" Tom pointed at a freight train moving through Winnipeg toward the trestle. Three powerful headlights glared along the tracks, and the whistle blasted. "I was right about a train—look!"

Dietmar looked at the train, then continued crossing the trestle. "I can reach the other side," he called.

Tom glanced across the river at Juba Park, where his suspect was moving out of sight, then he looked at Dietmar who was still crossing the trestle—moving with less confidence now. The tracks beneath him were shivering with the weight of the approaching train; the whistle was loud.

"Run, Dietmar," Tom yelled. "The train's coming fast! It's too heavy for the engineer to stop in time!"

The whistle screamed another warning as the huge train rumbled closer. Dietmar was now running toward the far side of the trestle, but his feet kept slipping. He yelled with terror.

Tom ran forward, shouting at Dietmar. "Jump," he cried. "It's your only chance! Jump into that snow!"

Below the trestle were heaps of snow, piled up for making sculptures. Dietmar glanced down at the snow, saw the huge engine coming closer, and jumped. He let out a cry as he plunged into a mound of white and disappeared. Tom watched anxiously for movement. After a few seconds, he saw Dietmar digging his way out from the pile of snow. White from head to foot, Dietmar resembled a mobile snowman as he stumbled down the river. Tom called his name, but Dietmar didn't reply.

* * *

Reaching The Forks, Tom spotted Charity near the rink with her father, Walt. "Have you seen Dietmar?" Tom asked, hurrying over to them.

"Yes!" Charity's dark eyes were wide. "He got his skates and headed for the bus. I called his name, but he pretended not to hear. He was covered in snow! What happened, Tom?"

He smiled. "Just a minor incident. Dietmar will be okay."

Charity turned to her father. "I bet they were after a suspect. Tom's a detective!"

"What happened, son?" Walt's eyes were red-rimmed today and he was frowning. He hadn't shaved, and his face was prickly with white bristles. "Were you chasing someone?"

"Sort of, I guess." Tom described his suspect and the theory about the gift statue. "There was a taller man in the attic as well. They're planning to hold the statue for ransom, I'm convinced of it."

"Say that code name again," Walt asked.

"Operation Golden Child." Tom studied his face. "Does that mean anything to you?"

Walt blinked. "Not a thing." Taking Charity's hand, he began walking toward the bus stop. "Coming home with us for some hot chocolate, Tom?"

Tom glanced at Charity. "That would be nice."

"Oh good," she said. "You can meet my kitten, Elvis. I gave him an unusual name to make him famous so he can maybe star in some TV commercials."

Walt nodded. "Yes, and earn some money."

Charity looked at her father with anxious eyes. He was silent on the bus all the way to their house in River Heights, the same neighbourhood that Tom lived in. Tom had a nice visit with Lassie, who belonged to the family. Walt made hot chocolate, which they drank at the kitchen table. Charity's brother, Donald, was there. He was a pale boy of six, with black hair and tired eyes.

"How are you feeling these days, Donald?" Tom asked.

"Not very good. I'm hoping to try a new medicine from the United States, but it costs a lot of money."

"I'm starting a campaign for funds." Walt held up a homemade poster. It showed Donald's face, and asked for donations. "I can't watch my son getting weaker. He's got to try that new medicine."

"Daddy, it's not guaranteed," Charity said. There was a deep crease between her eyes. "It's new and experimental . . . and very expensive. It might not work."

"We've got to at least try."

"I'll give some posters to my parents," Tom said. "They can display them at work."

"Thanks, Tom." For the first time that day, Walt smiled. "I'll go make two more."

"I'll help you, Dad," Donald said.

Charity left the kitchen with them, and returned carrying a photo album. "I'd like to show you this, Tom. It's the story of my family." The first picture showed her father, looking very young, outside a church with his bride. "They met in Churchill Falls, Labrador. They went to high school together. It's so cold in Churchill Falls that the centre of town is all indoors! The shops and schools and everything. Can you imagine that kind of cold?" She turned to a page that showed a baby's hospital picture, with the birth date written below. "That's me, I was born in Winnipeg. Cute baby, huh? I look like a little potato." She flipped to another picture. "Here's Daddy when he played Men's League basketball. Mom was the team's cheerleader."

"They're all such tall men," Tom said.

"Mr. Nicholson played on the team." Charity pointed at the picture. "There's Officer Rice. He was the coach." She turned the page. "And this is the last family picture in our album."

Tom looked at the date written beneath the picture. "That's several years ago. Why did the pictures stop?"

Charity sighed. "My parents separated just after this photo was taken . . ." Her voice trailed off. "Anyway, my mom moved out."

Tom watched her troubled face. "Where does she live now?"

"St. Boniface, in an apartment. She's got joint custody of me and Donald, so we spend most weekends with her."

"But not this one?"

Charity shook her head. "Mom's working at the arena this weekend. She juggles three jobs to make ends meet because she married young and didn't have any professional training, so . . . it's hard." Charity stroked her kitten's marmalade fur. "Isn't Elvis cute? Want to hold him?"

"Sure." The kitten throbbed in Tom's hand as he stroked the soft fur. "It's like he's got a motor inside! I should get one of these little guys."

Walt came into the room. "Here are the posters, Tom. Thanks for your help."

"You're welcome, Walt. Good luck raising the money."

Outside on the porch, Tom pulled on his toque. Light was fading from the afternoon sky, and the air was cold. "Do you think your dad can raise enough money in such a short time?"

"I don't know." Charity shook her head. "That so-called miracle medicine will cost a fortune, and Donald's condition is getting worse. Daddy's so stressed out, worrying about money." She managed a smile. "It was nice visiting with you, Tom. It took my mind off things."

Tom said goodbye, and walked toward the bus stop. He had homework to do.

* * *

Tom was soon downtown at the Public Library. He checked the notice board, in hopes that someone might be advertising for a detective, then made his way inside. A lot of people were there, selecting books from the shelves or reading at big tables. Browsing through the vertical file, he discovered a folder marked *Kidnappings* and took it to a study carrel.

Tom patiently worked through the collection of magazine and newspaper articles. Then, in the pile, he discovered a story written by Bryan Newgass several years earlier. Tom whistled in surprise—the headline on the story said *Manitoba girl kidnapped, wealthy parents ready to pay*. "This is like Dianne's kidnapping," he whispered, reading through the article. "I can't believe my eyes!"

Tom made notes, then found a pay phone and called his sister to tell her that he was running behind schedule.

"When will you be home, then?" Liz asked.

Tom looked at his watch. "Six-thirty—I haven't started my homework assignment yet. But I have run across some interesting information." Tom gave Liz details. "It happened up north in Flin Flon," he said. "Just like Dianne, the girl was taken away in a van. She had a personal security guard who shot one of the kidnappers in the leg, but they escaped with her."

"Why'd she have a personal guard?"

"Her parents ran the biggest mine in Flin Flon, so they had lots of money."

"What happened to the girl?"

"She was released safely after a big ransom was paid. The kidnappers were never arrested. I wonder if the same people grabbed Dianne?"

"Don't get yourself in trouble, Tom, let the police solve it. And don't be late coming home, Uncle Henry will have a fit."

"No sweat."

At the vertical file, Tom found the *Impaired Driving* folder and returned to his study carrel. Then his eyes bulged in surprise. The first article had the headline *Kennedy goes to prison.* "This is about Charity's father," he whispered to himself as he read. "Walt was jailed for drunk driving! He forced a family's car off the highway—the people might have been killed. It was his second offense." Tom couldn't believe it! It didn't sound like the Walt he knew at all.

Tom's mind was racing as he put the file back in place and hurried out of the library. "I wonder if Uncle Henry will take me to the hockey game tomorrow night?" he thought. "Then I could meet Charity's mom and try to find out more about Walt."

* * *

Winnipeg was playing Montreal that Sunday, so it was standing-room only. Jammed against a concrete wall, Tom and Uncle Henry joined in the excited cries as the teams stormed onto the ice, ready for the coming contest.

"I'll get us some hot dogs," Tom said, slipping away before his uncle could protest. "Be right back."

At the first convenience stand he found, Tom asked for Hilda Kennedy. "The only Hilda I know is Hilda McCracken over at the southwest hot dog stand," a man replied, gesturing with his hand. "Down there."

Tom decided to check it out. At the stand, he found three women in aprons waiting for customers. "Hilda McCracken?" he asked, stopping at the counter.

"That's me," a woman replied. She had crinkly hair that was turning grey. Her smile reminded Tom of Charity. "How can I help you?"

Tom was uncertain how to proceed. "My name's Tom Austen and I'm a friend of your daughter, Charity. Mr. Kennedy is the custodian at my school," he said. "I was at the festival yesterday with Charity."

"That's nice," Hilda McCracken said. "I'd like to take Charity and her brother to more things, but I'm so busy working. I've got three jobs, you see."

"Yes, I know," Tom said. "I met your son, Donald. I'm sorry that he's so sick."

"Yes . . . I'm working hard to save money to help him."

"I'm going to organize a fundraiser at school," Tom said. Then he hesitated. He wanted to learn more about Walt, but wasn't sure how to ask without seeming too nosy. "Walt's also trying hard to raise money for Donald's medicine," Tom said, finally. "Charity says that he wishes you two could work together."

"Walt's too proud to call me, so he sends messages through my daughter. Charity wants us to get back together, you see," she smiled. "Walt's a good man. But I'm afraid he would do just about anything to raise that money."

A roar of cheers rolled into the corridor from the rink. "Winnipeg just scored," Hilda McCracken said. "That means we'll be getting some hungry fans."

As the first excited faces appeared in the corridor, Tom smiled at her. "It was nice to meet you finally."

"Likewise, Tom. Thanks for being a friend to Charity. I know she's always cheerful, but life's hard for her. We all need support at times."

5

That night, Tom couldn't sleep. He tossed and turned, reviewing everything that had happened in the last few days. He was certain he knew the identity of the tall man he'd seen in the attic. Severe suspicions were forming in his head and he wanted to talk to somebody, so the next morning he went to his sister. Liz suggested talking to an adult, but Uncle Henry wasn't the right person. Then who?

On his way to school, Tom made a decision. He would talk to his teacher. He found Mr. Price in the classroom talking to Mr. Stones.

"Ah, Tom," Mr. Stones said, rattling coins in his pocket. "Have you finished reading my treatise on Sherlock Holmes?"

"Yes, sir. I learned some neat stuff!"

Mr. Stones smiled. "Mr. Price and I are very fortunate. We're both attending today's ceremony at the Legislative Building."

"I'd give anything to attend that ceremony and see all the security," Tom said, not mentioning his conspiracy theory.

Mr. Stones gave him a sympathetic smile as he left the classroom. "It's a shame there isn't an extra ticket available."

Tom walked toward Mr. Price. "Sir, something is really bothering me."

Mr. Price looked concerned. "What's wrong?"

"I think Walt may be involved in a crime, sir."

"This is serious," the teacher said, putting down his pen. "Why do you say that, Tom?"

Tom quickly described what he had overheard in the attic and how he felt he knew the tall man. "His voice was muffled and low, but seemed familiar."

Mr. Price listened intently.

"When I was doing my homework at the library, I ran across a clipping about Walt. He has a criminal record. He's been in prison! With him desperate for money and all, well . . . maybe *he's* the tall man."

"What would Walt's motive be? Money for Donald's medicine?"

"That's right, sir!"

Mr. Price studied Tom's face. "Listen Tom, all the teachers know about Walt's conviction for drunk driving. But Walt says he's never taken a drink since then, and I believe him. He's paid his debt to society. I don't think you should get too worked up about this."

"But Mr. Price, even his wife says he would do just about anything to get the money for Donald's medicine."

"When do your parents return to Winnipeg?"

"They're expected Wednesday, sir."

"That's only two days, Tom, so wait and discuss your concerns with them." Mr. Price looked toward the door. "Here come the other kids. I've got some good news."

"But what about the statue? I'm positive someone is going to steal it!"

"Tom, I hardly think that's possible. There will be a lot of security, trust me. Now, take your seat."

When everyone was seated, the teacher smiled. "I'm pleased to announce that we've now received permission for our special trip. We'll be travelling north on the *Prairie Dog Central*."

Excited cheers broke out.

"You'll need to bring sleeping bags," the teacher said. "Everyone will be billeted overnight with families in the town of Muskeg, then the train will return the next day to Winnipeg. You'll remember that Sadie Cheechov, our exchange student, lives in Muskeg, so we'll all get to see her again."

"Hey, sir," Dietmar said. "Does that mean you've cancelled our other field trip?"

"You mean to the Planetarium? No, we're still going."

"Great! Two days this week with no school!"

Christian Evans raised his hand. "Did you hear, Mr. Price? Lassie might be banned from the school."

"Our mascot? Whatever for?"

"Mr. Nicholson says she might have fleas. He's afraid parents will complain."

Mr. Price sighed. "Our principal is going through a rough time—please don't blame him for the decisions he's making. It's all because of Dianne's kidnapping. I'll talk to him after school. I'm sure he won't really do it."

Mr. Stones appeared at the door. "Excuse the interruption," he said to Mr. Price. "A meeting has come up, so I'm unable to use my invitation to the ceremony today at the Legislative Building. Is there anyone else that you would like to take?"

Tom's hand flew into the air. "May I go to the ceremony, sir? Please!"

Mr. Price shook his head. "Sorry, Tom. It's just not possible."

"But sir, I'd give anything to see the gift statue close up—plus all that security! I'll make a million notes and report to the class!"

Charity looked at Mr. Price. "That would be great, sir."

"Absolutely no way," the teacher replied. "Tom would be searching everywhere for clues. I don't want to be chasing after him during the ceremony."

"Come on, sir," Dietmar said. "Let Austen attend the ceremony, then he'll discover his conspiracy theory is a lot of hot air. We'll get a good laugh."

As the other students joined in, supporting Tom, Mr. Price threw up his hands. "Oh, good grief! All right, Tom, I'll take you to the ceremony. But you have to promise to behave!"

Tom grinned. "You can count on me, Mr. Price."

* * *

After completing his patrol duties, Tom waited for Mr. Price to finish working at his desk. Dietmar was also in the room, paying his penalty for constant horseplay. His task was to memorize a speech by Shakespeare, then write it down without looking at the play.

Tom grinned at Dietmar. "What are you memorizing?"

"It's something about to be or not to be. How can I learn words that don't make sense?"

Mr. Price looked at his watch. "You're lucky today, Dietmar. We're late for the ceremony at the Legislative Building. You're released."

With a whoop of joy, Dietmar raced into the hallway.

Mr. Price and Tom left the school and walked over to pick up the teacher's car at his home on Waterloo Street.

"Mr. Nicholson promised not to ban Lassie from the school, Tom," Mr. Price said. "He was just threatening, but he's calmed down now."

"That's great news, sir," Tom said, as they reached the teacher's home. "By the way, I was wondering if I could be billeted with Sadie's family when we go north? We got along really well when she was here."

"I'll see what I can do," Mr. Price answered.

After a short drive, they arrived downtown. Far above the Legislative Building, the Golden Boy glowed against the winter sky.

"Look at the security," Mr. Price said, parking the car. "Nobody could possibly steal the gift statue."

"I didn't expect all these officers and police dogs and guns," Tom said, "I guess my theory's a dud."

Mr. Price patted Tom on the back. "Let's go see the statue. That should be interesting."

After passing through the security checkpoint, they entered the building's main lobby, where the ceremony would be held. Stone walls reached high above to a large skylight. Sunlight streamed down on statues of two enormous buffaloes, guarding a wide staircase. Tom and Mr. Price were escorted to hard-backed chairs. They had a good view of the speaker's microphone and a table where the golden statue glittered inside a glass case.

"It's fabulous," Tom whispered to Mr. Price. "I bet that's shatterproof glass with a built-in alarm system."

The teacher nodded. "I don't think robbers would stand a chance."

"You're probably right." Looking up at an arch, Tom spotted the stone face of a woman with snakes around her face. "Wow. Who's that?"

Mr. Price glanced up. "Her name's Medusa. She . . ."

The teacher was interrupted by the arrival of the important guests, who were shown to comfortable chairs near the statue. "There's Dianne's father," Mr. Price whispered, pointing to a man with thinning hair.

"Why's he sitting up there, sir? He's not a politician."

"Because the Dorchesters are rich and powerful citizens of Manitoba."

Speeches began, and Tom was soon bored. He studied each face in the room, searching for criminals, but somehow he knew a heist was impossible. All around the walls stood armed police, and others watched from the staircase and doors. He had to admit it—the statue was safe.

* * *

When the ceremony was over, refreshments were served in the lobby. Tom swallowed a couple of free juices and ate some doughnuts. Then he wandered over toward the gift statue where it stood in its glass case. He stared into the eyes of the Golden Boy, then looked across the lobby at Mr. Dorchester.

Something strange was happening.

The wealthy industrialist had been surrounded by bodyguards when he arrived for the ceremony. But Mr. Dorchester was suddenly alone, and heading for the door. In his hand was an attaché case. As he went outside, Tom hurried to his teacher.

"Did you see that, sir?"

"See what?"

"Mr. Dorchester just left without his security guards. Isn't that strange behavior? I think something might be up."

Mr. Price looked at his watch. "It's probably nothing, Tom. I've got to make a phone call, then let's head home."

"I think I'll see where Mr. Dorchester's going."

"Tom, I am ordering you to stay put—or else!"

As the teacher hurried away to find a phone, Tom looked at the outside door. Surely it wouldn't hurt to have a quick look, just in case Mr. Dorchester got in trouble or needed help.

Tom glanced at the golden statue a final time, then

went to the door. Mr. Dorchester was walking past a small crowd that had gathered outside. The next thing Tom saw made his heart stop. A man in the crowd was watching Dianne's father while talking on a cellular phone, and he wasn't a security guard.

It was Rex—the same person who had followed Dianne in the pickup truck.

* * *

Racing through the lobby, Tom found Mr. Price. "Sir," he exclaimed. "I need your help! One of the kidnappers is here!"

"Not again! I thought I told you . . ."

"This is for real, sir!"

Mr. Price stared at him. "I wish I'd never brought you to this ceremony, Tom."

"Please, sir. I'm sure I just saw one of the kidnappers. Follow me, I'll prove it!" Tom ran through the crowd, with Mr. Price in pursuit.

"Tom Austen, come back here!"

Outside in the cold air, Tom pulled on his toque and gloves as Mr. Price reached his side. "There's the guy," Tom said, pointing. "He looks exactly like Rex, the man in the pickup who shadowed Dianne. Please, can't we check him out?"

"Absolutely not. This is a matter for the police."

As the man walked away, Tom stared in shock. "He's limping!"

"Why's that important?"

"Remember, the man I saw at the mystery house had a limp. Now things are starting to make sense!"

"Not to me," Mr. Price said, "so you'd better explain."

"It was Rex I saw in the attic. I thought those men were plotting to steal the statue, but I was wrong. Remember I told you they called it Operation Golden Child?"

Mr. Price nodded.

"That never meant the statue, sir. They were planning a kidnapping, not a robbery. Golden Child is their code word for Dianne! I bet Mr. Dorchester has the ransom in his attaché case."

"I doubt it, Tom."

"We'd better talk to the police, sir. This is for real."

"Have you got enough evidence to back up your theory?"

Tom thought for a moment. "Yes—for sure they should question Rex . . . Look, he's following Dianne's father. Come on sir, we've got to warn Mr. Dorchester!"

"Tom, come back here. That man could be dangerous."

"I'm okay, sir. I can follow Rex myself and take the bus home."

Mr. Price shook his head. "I'll go with you, Tom, but I think we're probably on a wild goose chase."

With the teacher beside him, Tom hurried through the darkness after Rex. Rush-hour traffic was crawling across a bridge over the Assiniboine; some people in cars were talking on cellular phones, others were sipping coffee. The sidewalks were busy, but there was no sign of Mr. Dorchester.

Tom looked at his teacher. "Want to hear my theory?" He continued without waiting for an answer.

"Attending that crowded ceremony gave Mr. Dorchester the perfect chance to sneak away from his bodyguards, maybe to meet Rex. That man is one of the kidnappers, I'm convinced of it."

"I've been thinking about it, Tom, and you may be right. You're the only one who knows what Rex looks like. Come on, let's get my car and drive to police headquarters. You can make a full report."

"Look, sir!" Tom pointed across the street at a bookstore. "Rex just went in there." He looked up at the traffic light. "Green at last. We'd better hurry, Mr. Price."

Headlights shone on their faces as they approached the bookstore. Through the window, Tom saw Rex thumbing a magazine near the cash register. Was he planning a holdup? "There's Mr. Dorchester!"

Dianne's father stood beside a shelf of paperbacks. He glanced at his watch, then returned a book to its place and quickly left the store, rushing past Tom and Mr. Price. Tom called out after him, but he didn't respond. "He's getting into a taxi," Tom said. "But look! He deliberately left his attaché case behind—I can see it beside that paperback shelf. I bet the ransom's inside. We'd better do something, sir."

Mr. Price pointed to a nearby pay phone. "I'll call 911. Wait right here, Tom. Don't go inside. It could be very dangerous."

"Yes, sir."

Looking in the window, Tom saw Rex walk through the store to the paperback shelf, and pick up the attaché case. Then he hurried toward the door where Tom stood.

Mr. Price was too far away to help, so Tom stepped into the bookstore and blocked the door. "Stop!" he said, raising his hand.

Rex hesitated. "Get out of my way," he snarled.

Tom glanced toward the cash register. A man behind it was watching them. "Sir," Tom called to him, "please phone the police."

Rex laughed harshly. "What is this?"

He tried to shove past Tom, who pretended to stumble. "My ankle," he shouted. "Help me, someone!"

Several customers stared at him. As Rex looked their way, Tom knocked the attaché case out of his hand and kicked it toward a customer. "Get that case," Tom cried. "There's a ransom inside!"

The man from the cash register started running toward them. Rex swore, then broke for the door. Outside the window, Mr. Price was walking toward the store. "Grab him, sir," Tom cried. "He's a kidnapper for sure!"

Mr. Price stared in shock as Rex dashed from the store. The teacher put out a hand to seize the criminal, but Rex knocked him aside and ran into the street. A pickup truck pulled up and he jumped into the passenger seat. Tom tried to see the driver, but his view was blocked by the truck's camper. He could only watch as the truck roared away.

* * *

"Did you call the police, sir?" Tom asked Mr. Price.

"The pay phone was broken, but . . ." Mr. Price raised his head. "Sirens."

"The police are coming! The man in the bookstore must have phoned."

Tom went inside with his teacher. The customers were talking with great excitement as a woman opened the attaché case. "It's full of money," she exclaimed. "I've never seen so much cash." The woman turned toward Tom. "There's the boy who started it all! What's going on?"

"Yeah," a man said. "What's all this money doing in a bookstore?"

"Well," Tom said, "I think Mr. Dorchester was ordered to leave the attaché case here for Rex to pick up. Then . . ."

The man from behind the cash register interrupted. "Better wait to be questioned by the police. Here they come." He looked out at a patrol car that screeched to a stop with its siren screaming and lights flashing. Two young officers jumped out.

As Tom and Mr. Price told the officers about Rex, another police car arrived, carrying Inspector Rachel Elberg and Officer Leonard Rice. Towering over Tom, Officer Rice demanded to know what was going on. "Tom, you are getting into things you shouldn't get involved in."

Mr. Price wagged his finger under Officer Rice's nose. "Tom's been a real help. If he hadn't been so alert, the kidnapper would have escaped with all that cash."

Inspector Elberg smiled at Tom. "So, you've found a genuine case at last. Congratulations."

"Don't encourage him, Rachel," Officer Rice said, "Tom could be in a lot of danger."

Tom wasn't afraid. He was thrilled. "Will my picture be in the newspaper?"

Officer Rice shook his head. "I'm afraid not." He looked at the other people. "I want secrecy from you all. These events mustn't become public knowledge yet."

"Fine," one customer said, and the others nodded. "Anything to help find Dianne Dorchester."

When the questioning ended, Tom and Mr. Price crossed the bridge toward the Legislative Building. "Do you think the kidnappers will try again for the ransom, sir?"

Mr. Price pondered the question. "No, Tom," he said at last. "They'll give up their plan and release Dianne. They took a big gamble kidnapping her, but it didn't work out. I think they are probably long gone. Why take another chance on getting arrested when they risk going to prison?" He shivered. "It's cold out tonight. Think about prison, Tom, what it would be like."

"I've . . ."

"The steel bars." Mr. Price shook his head. "Trapped in there day after day. No light, no freedom."

Back at the Legislative Building, Mr. Price unlocked his car. "Let's get the heater going. I can't stop shivering."

"It's delayed shock," Tom said. "I learned about it in a detective reference book. The medical part was *really* interesting, and now I'm reading about poisons. Some of them have really gross effects—cyanide, for example."

Mr. Price sighed. "Tom, you are really something."

* * *

The next day at school, Tom wanted to talk about the attempted ransom payment, but that was classified police information. The hardest moment came when Dietmar mentioned the golden statue.

"Was it stolen, Austen?" he asked sarcastically. "Was there a major heist?"

Tom continued to work at his desk, ignoring Dietmar.

"Well, Austen? Why'd we chase that guy all over St. Boniface? He wasn't a crook, and I nearly got killed!"

Charity looked at him. "It was your idea to cross the trestle, Dietmar."

Mr. Price stared at them from his desk. His eyes were tired. "Cut the noise, please. Dietmar, leave Tom alone—he's a more successful detective than you think."

As everyone returned to work, Tom gave Dietmar a smug look. Then he received a note from Charity asking to borrow his book of cryptograms, but when he looked in his desk, the book was missing.

"I've searched my desk," he told Charity at recess as they ate oranges together. "It was there just yesterday. I'm going to look for it after school patrol this afternoon."

"I'll help, if you want."

"Thanks, Charity."

Mr. Price joined their search after school, but the book was nowhere to be found. Soon Charity left, and Tom continued to look while the teacher did some marking. "I don't get it, Mr. Price. Why would anyone steal my book of codes?"

"I've no idea, Tom." Mr. Price took a sip of coffee, then rubbed his eyes. "Teaching is hard work. Some days I go home feeling completely exhausted." As he returned to his marking, the teacher's elbow struck the coffee mug. It fell off the desk and shattered on the floor. "Darn! I've broken my favorite mug."

"I'll get Walt, sir."

"No, don't bother him. I'll clean up the mess." Mr. Price started to pick up the pieces. "This isn't working. Tom, please do me a favour. Walt has a broom and dust pan in the boiler room. Would you get them for me?"

"Sure, Mr. Price."

"They're in the big cupboard where he keeps his cleaning supplies."

Tom hurried through the school. It seemed strange, deserted of kids and teachers and noise. Walt wasn't in the boiler room, but Tom quickly found the cupboard where the cleaning supplies were kept.

"Hey," he said, looking inside. "Here's my code book!"

It was lying on a shelf to the left of the broom. As Tom lifted it, a piece of paper fluttered to the ground. Written on it were some numbers:

7 18 1 2 / 11 9 4 / 4 5 20 5 3 20 9 22 5

The book was open to the simplest code, in which A was represented by the number 1, B was replaced by 2, and so on through the alphabet. Tom quickly copied the numbers into his notebook. "Let's see," he whispered, "7 is a G, 18 is an R, then A and B." He stared at the paper. "Gosh, the first word is GRAB."

Just then footsteps sounded behind Tom. He looked up, and saw a huge man looming above. It was the principal, Mr. Nicholson. "What's going on here?" he demanded.

Tom stammered. "Nothing, sir. I, uh, was just getting the broom and dust pan." Tom grabbed them and the cryptogram book and hurried out of the boiler room. Racing to his classroom, he handed Mr. Price the cleaning supplies, and then dropped into his chair and began decoding the numbers on the paper.

By the time Tom finished, his eyes were bulging in surprise. "Hey, Mr. Price," he called to his teacher, "I just found a code in the boiler room. Guess what it says? GRAB KID DETECTIVE." He stared at the words. "That means me. *I'm next!*"

6

Mr. Price stared at Tom. "Check the code again."

Quickly, Tom worked over the cryptogram. "The same words, sir. GRAB KID DETECTIVE."

"And you found it in the boiler room?"

"Yes, sir!"

"Then we'd better talk to Walt."

Mr. Price led the way to the boiler room. The big furnace whistled and groaned as it worked hard against winter's cold. Walt was repairing a shovel at his workbench.

Mr. Price showed him the paper with the code. "Is this yours, Walt?"

The caretaker shook his head. "I've never seen it before."

"Tom found it in your cupboard."

Walt's eyes flickered between Mr. Price and Tom. "What's wrong? Why are you both staring at me?"

Mr. Price gave his arm a friendly squeeze. "It's okay, Walt, just relax. These numbers could be a secret code, but nobody's accusing you of anything."

"A code? What do you mean?"

Mr. Price smiled at him. "Hey, relax, it's nothing. I'm sorry we've upset you." He turned to Tom. "Let's go."

Upstairs, Tom pulled on his winter clothes. "I can't believe Walt wrote that code," he said to Mr. Price.

"I agree," the teacher replied. "Maybe someone planted it as a gag."

Tom snapped his fingers. "Dietmar Oban! I bet he's the turkey who did it."

Boiling with thoughts of revenge, Tom went outside. The air was cold and pinched his skin. As Tom started walking, Walt called after him.

"Wait a minute, Tom," he said, pulling on his parka. "I want to ask you some questions."

"Sure, Walt." Tom was a little nervous, despite himself.

"I'm upset about that code." Walt's red-rimmed eyes gazed at Tom. "Was it about the kidnapping?"

"Possibly," Tom replied.

"What did it say?" the caretaker demanded.

Tom hesitated. "Well, I . . ."

"Tell me!"

"The code said GRAB KID DETECTIVE. But I'm sure it was just a gag."

"You're wrong!" Walt slammed one fist into the other. "Someone's setting me up. I'm going to get nailed for Dianne's kidnapping."

"I don't understand," Tom said.

The caretaker stared at him. "I've got a prison record, and Dianne attended my school. It was certain to happen—I'm going to get blamed for taking her. Someone left the code in the boiler room to make me look like a kidnapper." His eyes were desperate. "But I'm innocent, Tom. I never did it!"

* * *

The next day, Tom was still in turmoil about Walt and the cryptogram. It was probably Dietmar, but it *could* have been Walt. If only his parents would get home! Everyone—Mr. Price, Liz, Uncle Henry—said to wait for their advice before acting on any of his suspicions.

When Tom reached school, Charity said her father had stayed home from work. "His nerves are shot," she told Tom. "He thinks he's being set up for Dianne's kidnapping, and he's scared that *I'll* be kidnapped. Plus, he's trying to raise a fortune for Donald's medicine. Daddy's so unhappy these days."

Saying goodbye to his friend, Tom walked slowly toward the principal's office. He was heartsick that Walt might be involved in the kidnapping, but had to tell someone, just in case he disappeared as well!

"I'm not sure that Walt left the cryptogram," Tom said, after recounting his story to Mr. Nicholson, "but I'm worried that I may be next on the kidnapper's list. Walt does have a prison record, after all. Maybe he's hiding out today."

Light flashed from the principal's glasses as he studied Tom. "Walt's sick at home," he said. "That's hardly hiding out." He picked up the phone. "However, I'll discuss the matter with the police."

"Thanks, sir."

After a long discussion, Mr. Nicholson hung up the phone. "Officer Rice tells me that Walt is already a suspect because of his prison record. However, he has an iron-clad alibi for the time of the kidnapping."

Tom felt better. "Then that jerk Dietmar Oban was the one who set me up with the cryptogram."

"Or somebody else," Mr. Nicholson said, standing up. "The question is, who?"

* * *

Later that morning, Tom's class stepped out of a school bus at the Planetarium. As they shivered in the cold, Mr. Price lectured them about proper behavior.

"Please, sir," Dietmar cried, "let's go inside—I'm turning into an ice sculpture."

"Don't waste your time," Tom said. "I can already see through you." As others laughed, he added, "Especially your little game with the fake code."

"I already told you, Austen, I didn't do that."

Charity glanced at Tom. "He sounds serious."

Tom shook his head. "Nobody, but nobody, tricks Tom Austen. Dietmar's time is running out. Revenge will be mine, and it will be sweet." He wanted to sound sure of himself, but he was starting to think Dietmar was telling the truth.

Inside the Planetarium, the students peeled off various layers of outdoor clothing. "It's too bad my Dad's at home," Charity told Tom. "He was really looking forward to this show about dinosaurs. They're his big hobby."

"What's he got—the flu?"

Charity shook her head. "Just nerves, like I said. He needed the day off work, plus he's developing a new money-making scheme. The fundraising is taking longer than Dad expected."

Mr. Price called for quiet as the class was ushered into a circular auditorium. "Oh, wow," someone exclaimed. "What a place!"

The chairs all faced the center of the circle. Those nearest the front were slanted, allowing a good view of the dome above, where clouds trailed across a blue sky.

"This is like a dentist's chair," Dietmar complained, "but at least there's a view."

"It gets better," Mr. Price said. He turned to Mike Johnson. "Glad we're here, Mike? I know you're a dinosaur fan."

"You bet." Mike's eyes shone. "This is great."

Tom sat down beside Charity. "Sometimes my uncle comes here for concerts of recorded music combined with a laser show."

Mr. Price called for attention. "Today we'll be learning a theory about the fate of the dinosaurs. By the way, 'dinosaur' comes from two Greek words meaning terrible lizard."

"Will that be on a test, sir?" Flo Connolly asked. "Do we have to make notes?"

"No," Mr. Price replied. "Today you can just relax. Many dinosaurs lived in Alberta—there's a terrific museum of paleontology at Drumheller. Scientists still argue over why the dinosaurs disappeared." He smiled at Tom. "Too bad there wasn't a dinosaur detective taking notes sixty-five million years ago."

As the dome turned dark, a voice welcomed them to the show. Then a strange object rose slowly in the center of the room. It resembled a gigantic, two-headed praying mantis. Tiny lights were projected from it, filling the dome with a night sky of glowing stars and planets.

Pictures on the dome then took the students on a journey to the most distant planet of our solar system. From the barren surface of Pluto, they looked at the sun, now just a faint circle of light, before continuing to wander through space.

"We're entering the asteroid belt," the voice said, as a picture showed a huge chunk of rock passing by. "That one is ten kilometres in width, small for an asteroid." There was a dramatic pause. "But imagine the disaster if it crashed into our planet."

They were seeing an Alberta of ancient times. A flying reptile crossed the sky on wings of leathery skin. The scaly head of a brontosaurus rose above the trees. Munching on leaves, the huge lizard didn't notice the asteroid rushing closer and closer from space. Then it struck, crashing into Earth with a massive explosion.

"Clouds of dust filled the sky," the voice explained. "Night came, and took away the sun. For years and years, there was winter everywhere."

A stegosaurus trudged wearily across a frozen landscape. "That looks as cold as our schoolyard," Dietmar said, but nobody laughed. They were all misty-eyed as they watched eternal winter take away the last of the dinosaurs.

"Eventually, the skies cleared of dust," the voice said, "and new life began. Some scientists believe that birds are the direct descendants of dinosaurs."

A picture showed the outline of an enormous crater.

"Here's the evidence that something once hit Earth very hard. Was it an asteroid? If so, many scientists believe the Chicxulub Crater in Mexico is where it struck."

Back in the lobby of the Planetarium, the entire class demanded lunch before visiting the Ukrainian Centre. "Let's go to Chinatown," Flo suggested. "It's my favourite."

Mr. Price shook his head. "No, we'll go to Portage Place."

"But Chinatown's right across the street."

"We're not going there," the teacher said.

"Let's have a vote," Dietmar cried. "Who's for Chinatown?"

Everyone put up their hand, except for Mr. Price. "Okay," he said, "but let's make it fast."

With a cheer, the students began to put on their winter clothes. As Tom adjusted his toque, he heard someone hollering Charity's name, and turned to see Walt running across the lobby. "Charity," the man shouted, "are you okay?"

"Sure, Dad." She looked around in embarrassment. "What's wrong?"

Walt hugged his daughter. His face was red, and he was puffing for air. "I ran across town. I was so upset. Someone phoned . . . wouldn't give his name . . . said you were in danger."

Charity squeezed her father's hand. "I'm okay, Dad.

We're having lunch in Chinatown. Come with us, okay?"

"You bet I'll come," Walt said grimly. "You need me there to protect you."

Mr. Price smiled. "The kids are safe, Walt. But please join us."

A cold wind was blowing as they crossed Main Street to Chinatown. The weak sun lit colourful stores, with names displayed in Chinese and English; on signs above, dragons and jade trees glowed in neon, advertising restaurants that offered dim sum and Szechwan delicacies. Despite the cold, Chinatown was busy with shoppers going store to store, collecting supplies for the evening meal.

"Smells good," Dietmar said, pausing at the door of a grocery store. "I'm thinking of learning how to cook Chinese food. I may specialize in dim sum."

Tom laughed. "Good idea, Oban. You sure are some dim."

Charity studied a variety store's crowded window. "Look at the rosewood tortoise. It's a little box—isn't that neat?"

Tom noticed a joke section inside the store. "Let's look inside this place," he suggested, then turned to Mr. Price. "Which restaurant are we going to, sir?"

"I haven't decided yet. Let's just keep moving."

"I'm frozen," Mike Johnson protested. "Let's vote on a restaurant. How about that one across the street?" Hands went up everywhere. "It's settled!"

"We'll meet you there," Tom said.

Tom, Charity and Walt entered the long, narrow variety store. Paper lanterns hung from the ceiling, and a Chinese rock singer entertained on a TV screen.

As Walt hovered nearby, Tom and Charity explored the shelves and Tom made a purchase from the jokes section. Then they hurried across the street to the restaurant, where the other kids had filled all the booths, leaving the latecomers to join Mr. Price at a round table in the window. When he was seated, Tom looked across the street. Beside the variety store was another store selling groceries and a third that offered poultry. Above these stores were three floors of windows; several of the windows were filled with plants. A sign on the building said Hotel Rooms by the Week or Month.

"Do people live in that kind of hotel, Mr. Price?" Tom asked, gesturing toward the building.

"I don't know, Tom."

"It says 'rooms by the week or month.'"

"So it does."

"It would make a great hideout."

"No more detective work," Mr. Price snapped. "Or should I report you to Mr. Nicholson?"

"Okay, sir, I'm sorry." Tom raised both hands. "I'll never be a detective again."

Dietmar grinned from a nearby booth. "The criminals of the world can relax."

Tom went over to squeeze in beside Dietmar and the others. They were working through plates of steaming chow mein and deep-fried pork. "I'll demonstrate how to use chop sticks," Tom said, grabbing some from the table. "First of all . . ." Pausing, he gazed at Dietmar's plate. "What's *that*?"

Everyone stared.

"Is it a maggot?" Tom leaned closer. "No, worse! It's half a maggot. I can see its insides!" Quickly, he moved away from Dietmar. "You've been eating maggots, Oban. How disgusting!"

With a horrible moan, Dietmar stumbled from the booth and ran for the washroom. When he eventually returned, looking pale, everyone stared. Then Tom picked up the half maggot from Dietmar's plate and ate it.

"Candy maggots," he said, holding up his package from the variety store. "No more fake cryptograms, Oban, got that?"

Dietmar lunged, but was seized by an alert Mr. Price. Tom returned to his own table and dug into some food while he studied the hotel across the street.

"See that end window on the top floor? Isn't that a cellular phone leaning against the glass?"

"Tom," Mr. Price sighed. "Don't you ever quit?"

"But that guy Rex had a cellular phone. I remember seeing a star-shaped decal on it, just like that one in the window."

Mr. Price looked at the customers eating lunch. "Lots of people have cellular phones. I see several in here. Personally, I'd like them banned from restaurants. They are really distracting."

"I haven't eaten in a restaurant in ages," Walt said. "It's so expensive these days."

"I love going out for a meal," Mr. Price said. "Why aren't you eating now, Walt?"

"No appetite."

Outside in the cold, a familiar face was coming their way. "It's that TV reporter, Bryan Newgass," Tom exclaimed. "He's got a crew with him—a camera and everything."

"A reporter?" Walt stared at Bryan Newgass. "I don't

like this. Reporters can give people a rough time."

"Maybe they're coming for lunch," Charity suggested as the front door opened.

Mr. Price shook his head. "No, something's happened. I can tell by the look on their faces."

Bryan Newgass and his crew hurried to their table. "I've tracked you down," he told Mr. Price. "I need an interview!"

"Why? What's going on?"

Bryan Newgass pulled a small device from the pocket of his parka. "I listen to police calls on this scanner. Today, I hit the jackpot—less than an hour ago, a ransom was given to Dianne's kidnappers! Mr. Dorchester took the money to the cathedral in St. Boniface and a man escaped with it."

Tom turned to Charity. "On Saturday, I spotted Rex at the cathedral!" He looked at Walt, suddenly remembering that he had also seen him in St. Boniface the same day. He didn't want to mention that to Charity.

As the camera light glared, Bryan Newgass looked at the students. "I want some comments from you. How do you feel, knowing that Dianne's ransom has been paid and she may be coming home?"

Dietmar was quick to give his thoughts, but Tom refused. "Never again," he told Bryan Newgass.

The reporter suddenly turned to Walt. "Hey, I recognize you. Walt Kennedy, right? I covered your court case for a newspaper. Why are you here?"

"He's my dad," Charity said, clutching Walt's arm. "We're having lunch."

"Walt's the caretaker at our school," Mr. Price added. "Now leave us alone."

Bryan Newgass stared at Walt. "You're the caretaker at the school where Dianne Dorchester was kidnapped? That sounds odd to me, considering your past . . ."

Walt's red-rimmed eyes were huge. Sweat shone on his forehead and upper lip. "No . . ." he stammered. "I . . ."

Charity held her father tighter. "He'd never kidnap anyone!"

The reporter ignored Charity. "Say, Walt, you look mighty stressed. Where were you this morning? Got an alibi for when the ransom was collected?"

Walt's face shone in the harsh light of the camera. "I . . ." He opened and closed his eyes, blinking hard. Then he stood up, and grabbed his parka. "I'm going home."

"I'll go with you, Daddy," Charity said.

She grabbed her coat and hurried away with her father. Bryan Newgass and his crew also left the restaurant, eager to get their story to the TV station. As the other kids chattered excitedly, Tom began writing notes, trying to make sense of what was going on. He gazed up at the window across the street where he could see the cellular phone. How could he get a closer look at it?

* * *

Later that afternoon, the hotel window was again being studied from the Chinese restaurant. This time, the person who sat at the round table wore a blazer and grey flannel trousers; he was short and looked stout, although his face betrayed no fat. On his upper lip, a thin line suggested a moustache, and his eyebrows were unusually dark. On his head was a tartan cap from Scotland, pulled low. A waitress took his order without comment.

Satisfied with his disguise, Tom lifted a pair of small binoculars to his eyes. Now he could clearly see the cellular phone in the hotel window. *As I suspected,* he wrote in his notebook, *this could be the phone Rex had in the pickup truck. Same model, same colour, same decal.*

Tom drew a sketch of the hotel, highlighting the window where he could see the cellular phone. He drank some milk. The restaurant was very warm, and he was sweating inside his blazer. Around Tom's stomach were rolled-up towels to make him appear fat. His woolen trousers were itchy, and he began to worry about sweat smudging the eyebrow pencil he'd used to darken his brows and create his moustache.

Then, to his surprise, the principal of Queenston School came into the restaurant. Tom ducked his head, afraid his cover would be blown, but Mr. Nicholson didn't even glance his way. He hurried over to a corner booth where a man sat sipping tea from a small cup. The two men greeted each other warmly.

After they had ordered, Mr. Nicholson's companion opened an attaché case, took out some bills, and began counting. The two men looked pleased with each other—they made a toast and continued to talk excitedly.

Tom made notes, wondering what all the money was for. He couldn't hear what they were saying, so he finally decided it was time to continue his original mission. He went to the washroom and altered his disguise by changing ties, putting on sunglasses and hanging his left arm in a sling. Pretending to have a bad back, he moved slowly through the restaurant. Some people stared, but others seemed fooled. Mr. Nicholson and his friend didn't even look up.

Outside, it was growing dark. Thin, hard snow was being driven through Chinatown by an unfriendly wind. Tom shivered. He wanted to hurry, but he had to maintain his disguise. Putting a hand on his lower back, he slowly hobbled, as if in pain, across the street and entered the hotel.

Tom climbed to the top floor. He heard radios and TV sets and someone with a bad cough as he walked along the hallway toward the end room—the room that had the cellular phone in the window.

Summoning courage, Tom knocked on the door.

There was no answer, but Tom could hear someone moving inside. He knocked again, harder.

"Who's there?" a voice called.

"Um," Tom said, then raised his voice. "I'm selling the Canadian Junior Encyclopedia, door to door."

"I don't want any," the voice grumbled.

Tom knocked again. "We have a special you wouldn't want to miss."

The door flew open. Rex's little blue eyes stared at Tom. In his hand was the shadowy shape of a gun. "So, kid detective, we meet again." A wicked smile spread across Rex's face. "I spotted you over in the restaurant with your binoculars." Pulling Tom into the room, he slammed the door. "Who else knows about my hideout?"

"Nobody," Tom said miserably. "This was my idea. Please let me go."

"Forget it, I'm getting out of here and I could use a hostage." Rex grabbed the cellular phone from the windowsill, then shoved a package under his parka. "Let's get moving."

"Is the ransom in that package?" Tom asked, as Rex led him into the hallway.

"None of your business."

"Is Dianne safe?"

"Shut up."

They moved quickly down the dark hallway. Tom heard people talking behind some doors, but he knew an innocent person might get shot if he yelled for help. "Is Walt your partner?" he asked.

"Shut up, kid! I've got an itchy trigger finger."

With Tom beside him, Rex cautiously descended the stairs. They saw no one. In the lower hallway, Tom was led to the outside door. They stepped onto the busy sidewalk. Neon signs glowed red and green above their heads. In the harsh light, Tom looked at the gun in Rex's hand; it was plastic. "That's a fake," he exclaimed. Then he yelled, "Help me, someone!"

Rex spat a nasty word at Tom and waved the gun in the air. People screamed and dove for cover. Rex roughly pushed Tom to the ground, then hurried along the sidewalk and disappeared into a side street. Tom picked himself off the sidewalk, hesitated, then followed.

The street was dark and very narrow, with garbage dumpsters creating frightening shadows. Tom followed Rex's footprints in the snow, then bent down to make a snowball for protection. But he stopped. Suddenly, his heart leapt into his throat.

Somewhere, in the darkness, an engine roared. A garage door opened, headlights sprang to life and tires screeched against concrete. Tom looked desperately for cover.

A truck was coming his way, moving fast. It was Rex's pickup truck!

7

Tom threw the snowball and dove for cover in a narrow doorway.

The snowball splattered on the windshield in front of Rex, and the pickup went out of control. It bounced against a brick wall, throwing sparks, then headed for a garbage dumpster on the opposite wall. Rex managed to steer out of danger just in time and the truck raced into the street.

Distant sirens wailed in the air as Tom ran after Rex. The tires of the pickup screeched and the truck fled into the night. People were talking excitedly to each other, gesturing and pointing as the first police cars began to arrive.

In one car was Inspector Ted Austen of the Winnipeg City Police. "Dad," Tom cried, running toward him. "You're home at last!"

Mr. Austen hugged his son. He had the same black eyes and hair as his daughter, Liz. "We caught a last-minute flight out of Mexico. Officer Rice and Inspector Elberg met us at the airport, and brought me straight here."

"Mom's okay?"

Mr. Austen nodded. "We had a great time. Now, tell me what happened here—and what *are* you wearing?"

In the car, while his father listened intently, Tom recounted his story, going back to the first raid on the mystery house. "The worst thing is," he said, "evidence keeps piling up against Walt Kennedy. I keep trying to think of other explanations, then something else suspicious happens." He explained all his evidence to his father, and they discussed the different possibilities.

Later that evening, Tom told his story again at home to Liz and his mother. Judith Austen was a tall woman with flaming red hair and blue eyes. She was a criminal lawyer.

Uncle Henry said goodbye at the front door. His bags were packed and he was smiling. "Your kids are great," he told Mr. and Mrs. Austen, "but my nerves are frazzled. They're a little too adventurous for me!"

Tom and Liz said goodbye. "Remember your promise," Liz said to Uncle Henry. "If you get invited to Casa Loma, you'll take us along."

"Okay, but only if it's a peaceful visit."

"Tell us about Mexico," Liz said to her parents. "Did you hear any good superstitions?"

"Just one," Mrs. Austen replied. "Seeing a white dog

before noon means you'll have good luck that day."

Liz made a note. "That's a nice one for my files."

As they talked, Mr. Austen fielded a call from police headquarters. "Interesting information," he said, hanging up. "The ransom contained bills with consecutive serial numbers. Mr. Dorchester made a note of the numbers before leaving the money at the cathedral."

"Why, Dad?" Liz asked.

"He figured it would help us find the kidnappers— and it may be working. Banks and stores were warned right away to watch for the bills, and some have already started turning up."

"You know," Liz said, "this detective work is kind of interesting." She made some notes. "How do the marked bills help you, Dad?"

"They may tell us where the kidnappers are hiding out. The money has been spent in two neighbourhoods. One is Chinatown . . ."

"Where Rex was in hiding," Tom said.

Mr. Austen nodded. "And the other is our neighbourhood, River Heights."

Tom looked at him in dismay. "That's even more evidence against Walt. He lives in River Heights."

"But," Mr. Austen said, "as we've discussed, Walt's got a solid alibi for the afternoon Dianne was kidnapped. Besides, the marked bills aren't definite proof. A couple showed up in other parts of town."

"What happened to Rex?" Mrs. Austen asked.

"The driver of the pickup truck? Unfortunately, he escaped."

"So, you're after him, and the tall man from the attic. Any idea who he might be?"

Her husband shook his head. "Nothing definite—but we do have Tom's theory. We're keeping an eye on Walt, of course, but there is no concrete evidence against him. Someone could be setting him up, like he claims."

* * *

The next day, Tom sat beside Charity in the school bus on the way downtown to the railway station. Walt was in the seat behind, beside Mr. Price, who was bundled up in a blue parka with a fur-lined hood. They were on their way to the station to board the *Prairie Dog Central* for their special train journey to the north.

"The only sad thing," Tom said, turning around to speak to Walt, "is that Dianne is still missing. I can't understand why the kidnappers haven't released her." Watching Walt's eyes, he added, "They've got their ransom money, haven't they?"

"I guess so," Walt replied, "and they've probably spent it all by now."

"Do you think the kidnappers had a valid reason for needing the ransom?" Tom asked.

"Of course not. It belongs to the Dorchesters." Walt rubbed his hands together nervously. His eyes were puffy, and his voice shook. "I'm a wreck. I'm only coming on this trip to protect Charity."

Mr. Price looked at Walt. "Please don't worry, Walt," he said. "The kidnappers have their money. They won't strike again. Dianne will probably be released once they've escaped from Manitoba."

Mr. Stones led everyone in some camp songs, then

gave a humourous talk about the history of early Manitoba. It was easy to tell he was liked by the kids in his class. Outside the bus, snow was falling from the grey sky. The flakes were small, but numerous. People walking past on the sidewalk were huddled forward, heads into the wind.

Huge pillars rose up by the front door of the railway station. "Pioneers called Winnipeg the gateway to the west," Mr. Stones explained. "They came through here on trains pulled by old steam locomotives. The *Prairie Dog*'s locomotive was built in 1882 in Scotland, and it's still operating! This excursion train usually runs only in the summer, so we're lucky to be guests today."

The students grabbed their duffel bags and dashed through the cold. Inside the station, they found a festive scene. Banners and signs welcomed the Railway Pioneers of Manitoba to a celebration of their history. The station had become a temporary museum; there were conductors' hats, photos of old trains and newspaper articles about famous railway disasters. The station was filled with people, laughing and talking as they enjoyed refreshments, waiting to board the *Prairie Dog Central* for its special journey.

"This is neat," Tom said to Charity.

She nodded, but her worried eyes were on Walt. He was gazing across the station at the bright lights of a TV camera. Interviewing someone in its glare was Bryan Newgass.

"Not that reporter again," Walt hissed. "I'm getting out of here."

"But Daddy," Charity said, "you promised to come on the *Prairie Dog*."

"Then let's get on the train," Walt replied. "I don't want anything to do with that guy. I don't like him."

"He's busy, Daddy, and the station is crowded. He'll never notice you."

"Why don't you buy a coffee," Mr. Price suggested, "then we'll all get on board the train."

"Okay," Walt said, "that's a good idea."

Mr. Price smiled at Tom. "Great we're here, eh? It was lucky Mr. Stones knew about this special trip on the *Prairie Dog* to celebrate the pioneers."

They were interrupted by the approach of Bryan Newgass and his camera crew. "Great to see you again," the reporter exclaimed. He thrust a microphone under the teacher's nose. "Why is your class going on a train trip when Dianne is still missing? Don't you think the other kids may be in danger?"

Mr. Price pushed the microphone aside. "Leave us alone. We've had enough of your questions."

Mr. Nicholson approached. "Trouble, Mr. Price?" The principal leaned his face close to Bryan Newgass. The two tall men stood nose-to-nose, staring at each other. "Leave my staff and students alone," Mr. Nicholson said. "Is that clear?"

The reporter grinned. "Sure thing, fella. Nice talking to you."

As he turned to go, a woman approached. She had brown eyes, chestnut-coloured hair, and lots of shiny red lipstick. "I'm Carmilla Cain, reporter for the *Winnipeg Free Press*."

Bryan Newgass winked at her. "You're new, right? I know all the reporters at that newspaper, and I've never seen you before."

"Yeah, I just started."

Carmilla Cain paused. She was staring across the crowded lobby of the railway station at Walt. The caretaker was leaving the refreshment stand with a coffee. His shoulders slouched, and he looked unhappy.

"That man," Carmilla exclaimed. "I recognize him!" The reporter paused, while heads turned. "Someone arrest him. He's one of the kidnappers!"

* * *

With a cry of fear, Walt made a break for the street. Several people went after him. Bryan Newgass seized Walt just before he reached the door.

"Don't cause any trouble," the big reporter warned, then turned to the startled crowd. "Someone get the cops!"

"I'll call 911," a woman shouted.

Charity ran to her father's side and clutched him. "Don't hurt my father," she begged Bryan Newgass. "He didn't kidnap Dianne."

Mr. Nicholson put a comforting arm around Walt's shoulders. "Try to stay calm, so we can help." He turned to Carmilla Cain. "Why do you accuse Walt of being a kidnapper?"

"Because . . ." The woman hesitated, thinking. "Because I was on Wellington Crescent when Dianne Dorchester was kidnapped. I saw the man who pulled her into the van." She pointed at Walt. "It was you!"

"No," he whispered. "That's not true."

Suddenly, there was a shout from a man at the refreshment stand. "Hey, that guy gave me a bill from the ransom payment. I just checked the serial number." He stared at Walt. "You're passing the ransom money!"

"No," Walt cried. "No, no!"

With desperate energy, Walt tore free and ran. Bryan Newgass tried to seize him, but slipped. He fell, giving his knee a nasty smack on the marble floor. People helped him up, while others ran to the station door and watched Walt disappear down the street.

"That guy's escaping," a man yelled. "He's guilty for sure!"

"No," Charity said. Tears were streaming down her face. "It's just not possible!"

Sirens wailed outside and then police officers ran into the station. Statements were recorded, and the order was given to find Walt and take him in for questioning. Mr. Nicholson and the teachers tried to comfort Charity, who refused to continue on the excursion.

"I've got to be here for Donald and my folks." Charity turned to Tom before leaving the station. "Please, try to help my Dad. I know he's not guilty."

"I'll do my best," Tom replied. His heart ached for his friend.

All around, the crowd was wild with excitement. Bryan Newgass and the other reporters were busily collecting interviews, but Carmilla Cain just watched them.

"Why aren't you interviewing anybody?" Tom asked.

"I don't feel like it," she replied. "Seeing that guy run kind of upset me."

"But you're the one who accused him."

"I know, but still . . ." Her voice trailed off.

"Haven't you covered anything like this before?"

"Sure," Carmilla said. "But, I don't know, this just

scared me." She looked at Tom. "I'm going on the *Prairie Dog*. I'll interview you during the trip, okay?"

"Okay," Tom replied.

Mr. Nicholson and the teachers tried to convince the students to board the train, but everyone wanted to be interviewed. Only when the reporters left the station did the kids and the railway pioneers head for Track 2. Tom walked beside Mr. Nicholson, who was very upset about Walt's arrest. "He's a fine man and a dedicated father. Why would he kidnap Dianne Dorchester?"

Mr. Price glanced at the principal. "For money," he suggested. "His son needs that expensive medicine."

"But people are responding to his campaign for funds," the principal protested. "Enough money will be donated by the community."

"Yes, but how long will it take? Donald needs help immediately."

Mr. Nicholson shook his head. "I still don't believe Walt is a kidnapper." He looked at the reporter, Carmilla Cain, whose rucksack appeared heavy. "The way she fingered Walt for the kidnapping seemed fake to me."

"She could be telling the truth," Mr. Price said, then turned to Tom. "You're the detective around here. Does Carmilla Cain seem truthful?"

"I'm not sure," Tom replied. "Let's keep an eye on her."

"Good idea," Mr. Price said. "During the trip, we'll ask *her* some questions."

Tom turned to the principal, wanting to ask him what he had been doing in Chinatown and why his friend had given him some money, but he was too afraid. Instead, he looked Mr. Nicholson straight in the eye and said, "If Walt isn't the tall kidnapper, who is?"

Mr. Nicholson looked down at him. "I've no idea, Tom," he replied.

* * *

The *Prairie Dog Central* waited proudly on Track 2. The steam-powered locomotive was black with gold trim; behind it was the tender, where coal was stored to feed the big fire that made the steam. In his cab above, the engineer grinned and waved. "Hey, mister," he called to Mr. Price. "Climb up and have a look."

"Wow," Tom said. "Okay to go with you, sir?"

Mr. Price nodded. They climbed a steel ladder to the cab, where the engineer was shoveling coal into a roaring fire. "You've got to have steam," he said, checking a gauge. "This loco won't move without it. I'll show you how things work."

Mr. Price asked intelligent questions, impressing the engineer. "You've got an instinct for this loco. When you retire from teaching, join our society that operates the *Prairie Dog Central*."

"I'll think about that," Mr. Price replied.

"Thanks for the tour," Tom said. "It was great."

Back at the tracks, they followed Mr. Stones toward a passenger car. "This is Coach 101," he said as they climbed aboard. "It's a Pullman, built in 1910 for the Rio Grande Railroad."

A woman tugged on the teacher's sleeve. She was tiny and white-haired, with bright brown eyes. "Correction, young man," she said. "It was called the Denver and Rio Grande Western. I travelled on it with my late husband.

I've got an album full of pictures from our trip."

Mr. Stones smiled. "Would you bring them to our school for the kids to see?"

"Delighted to," she said, beaming with pleasure.

Two rows of seats ran the length of Coach 101, ending at a washroom and the door to the next car.

"Where's the refreshment booth?" Dietmar asked.

"You'll be served at your seat by an attendant called a News Butcher," Mr. Stones explained.

"Can we charge the food to you, sir?"

The teacher smiled. "You've got a great sense of humour, Dietmar."

"*All aboard!*" cried a voice outside.

With a lurch, the train started forward. Coal smoke drifted to their noses as the *Prairie Dog Central* moved slowly out of the station and then gathered speed. Cars honked, and people waved from office buildings as the train rolled proudly past, its whistle blasting a greeting.

"This is so exciting," a bald man with friendly eyes said to Tom. They sat across the aisle from each other. "I worked the railways all my life."

Tom chatted to the man and before long the city was gone, replaced by frozen prairie. The white land reached to the distant horizon. "The *Prairie Dog*'s summer run is to Grosse Isle," the man told Tom, "so it's exciting to be going to the far north for a change."

"How'd this train get its name?" Tom asked.

"When I was a boy, there were prairie dogs everywhere. Little rodents that live underground in burrows up to 80 feet in length. I guess the trains saw plenty of them."

Cinders from the smokestack blew past the window. Tom looked at a distant farmhouse, alone on the vast prairie. "I wonder how Walt's doing," he said to Mr. Price. "I wish I could phone Charity to see if she's okay."

"When we reach Muskeg," Mr. Price said, "you can use my telephone calling card to phone Charity."

"Thanks, sir."

For a long time, Tom was silent. He watched the scenery change from prairie to rolling, bushy country. But his mind was occupied with more than the scenery. He couldn't stop thinking about the case, especially Walt running from the station.

Then Mr. Price nudged his arm. "I've been watching Carmilla Cain, the so-called reporter. She hasn't written down a single thing."

The woman sat alone at the end of the coach. She looked at Tom, then pretended to gaze out the window. "She was supposed to interview me," he said, "but nothing's happened."

Mr. Price stood up. "Let's go talk to Carmilla Cain. I'm starting to feel really suspicious about her."

The coach swayed back and forth, making it difficult to walk. Tom and his teacher squeezed past kids who stood in the aisle talking to the pioneers, and sat down in the seat opposite the reporter. "Hiya," she said, yawning. "When do we get there, anyway?"

"It shouldn't be long." Mr. Price looked out the window. "We're in real bush country now."

Snow was falling on rolling hills covered with evergreens. In the distance was a white, frozen lake. Two cross-country skiers paused to wave at the train, then continued their adventure. As the News Butcher arrived selling candy, the *Prairie Dog Central* whistled past a tiny station. A group of train fans waited on the platform, braving the cold to wave.

"The next station is Muskeg," the News Butcher said, "but first we enter twenty kilometres of absolute wilderness. Let's hope the snow doesn't strand us."

It was much thicker now, whirling past the windows. Tom watched it fall on trees, rocks and bush. He turned to Carmilla Cain. "Where'd you get started as a reporter?"

"Um." The woman's eyes flickered to Mr. Price, then back to Tom. "Um . . . Flin Flon. Flin Flon is where I got started."

"Did you cover the kidnapping up there? It happened three years ago."

Mr. Price looked at Tom. "You know about that case?"

"Sure, sir. I did some research at the library."

"You're quite the sleuth." The teacher turned to Carmilla Cain. "Do you mind answering some questions?"

Her eyes narrowed. "What's the problem?"

"Nothing much, but Tom and I have some concerns."

"Meaning?"

"Well, quite frankly, we're wondering if you're really a reporter."

"What absolute nonsense," the woman replied, but she didn't sound convincing. Her eyes stared at Tom, then at Mr. Price.

"Do you carry an identification card?" the teacher asked.

"What are you talking about?"

"If you're a reporter for the *Free Press*—you must have a photo ID."

Carmilla Cain didn't reply. She studied her watch, then looked at the wilderness. In the distance was a high trestle that would take the train across a frozen river.

"Well," Mr. Price demanded. "What about it, Ms. Cain? Do you have an ID card?"

"Okay." Carmilla Cain reached inside her bulky parka. "Here's my ID, Mr. Nosy."

In her hand was a revolver. "It isn't plastic," she said to Tom. "This thing shoots real bullets. Don't give me any trouble."

* * *

Carmilla Cain stood up and pointed the gun at Tom and Mr. Price. Everyone screamed and ducked for cover.

"You'll make perfect hostages," she snarled. "And don't think I wouldn't shoot." She looked at the teacher. "We're going into the next coach. Lead the way."

There was snow between the coaches. Mr. Price's hand shook as he opened the door to the next car. The only person inside was the conductor, who sat looking out the window. "Sorry, folks," he said as they entered, "you're not allowed in here. The heating isn't working properly."

Carmilla Cain waved the gun at him. "Shut up, Mr. Conductor."

His eyes bulged. "What's going on?"

"Shut up."

Mr. Price pulled the fur-lined parka hood over his head. "It's cold in here. Let us go."

Carmilla Cain gave him a look of disgust. "You wimp—you'll be the first to die." She leaned close to the window. "We're almost at the trestle. The train will be making an unscheduled stop."

"Why?" the conductor asked.

"No questions," she hissed.

Creaking and groaning, the *Prairie Dog Central* came to a shuddering halt on the trestle. Snow tumbled toward a frozen river far below. "That's a long drop," Tom said, shivering.

Carmilla Cain smiled. "Care to try it, kid detective?" She pointed the gun at the conductor. "Go into Coach 101 and calm everyone down. Nobody should try to sneak off the train—it means instant death. Tell them I'll start shooting hostages if they don't behave."

"Yes, ma'am, I'll do that." Putting on his uniform cap, the conductor scurried out of the car.

The woman stared at Tom. "I've got a job for you." She pointed toward the far end of the coach. "That door leads to the locomotive. Go see the engineer—he's got a surprise waiting for you."

His legs numb, Tom walked quickly along the aisle and opened the door to outside. He looked at the winding white river far below as he climbed down to the tracks and worked his way forward past the tender. Steam hissed from the locomotive; the engineer sat in the open window of the cab. Tom called up to him, but the man didn't move. Cold snowflakes whirled past in the wind.

"Mr. Engineer," Tom called again. "There's trouble!" Seizing the steel ladder, he began climbing toward the cab. "My teacher's a hostage, and . . ."

Tom stared in horror. There was a gun pointed at the engineer's head. It was held by Rex.

* * *

"So, kid detective, we meet again." Rex smiled. Behind him, the locomotive's fire roared. "Climb down to the trestle, both of you."

"Are you kidnapping us?" Tom demanded.

"Shut up and get moving."

On the trestle, Rex led Tom and the engineer past the hissing locomotive. "This time, my gun's real," he said. "Don't try to escape. Understand?"

Tom nodded.

They reached the end of the trestle. Parked across the rails was Rex's pickup truck. "So that's why the train stopped," Tom said.

"You're a brilliant detective, kid."

"Why haven't you released Dianne?"

"Shut up." Rex gestured for Tom and the engineer to stop walking. "We're staying here."

Tom huddled deeper into his parka. They could see the river, far below. On the trestle, the *Prairie Dog Central* was motionless except for clouds of escaping steam. Tom saw faces watching them from the windows of the coaches.

"What's going to happen?"

"Quiet." Rex took out a radio phone. His breath turned white as he said, "Begin Operation Terminate."

"*Acknowledged*," a voice crackled from the speaker.

The door of the first coach opened and Carmilla Cain waved toward Rex with her radio phone. She stepped out of sight, and for a moment there was silence. Then a gunshot rang out. It echoed down the river valley, followed by a cry of horror. Tom stared in disbelief as a body tumbled from the train and fell toward the river. He recognized the blue parka and ski pants.

They belonged to his teacher, Mr. Price!

8

Tom turned away, stunned by the sight.

"*Hostage terminated*," a voice crackled from Rex's radio.

"Message received," he replied.

"But . . ." Tom couldn't make his voice work. "But . . ."

Rex gestured at the engineer with his gun. "Board the train, and get it moving when I signal—and take the kid detective with you."

"You killed my teacher! How could . . ."

"Move it!"

Thin flakes stung Tom's face as he walked along the trestle with the engineer. Neither one spoke, they were both in shock. Tom was barely aware that he was walking. The engineer escorted Tom to the first coach, then climbed into the locomotive.

Outside, the sky was growing dark. In no time at all, the train shuddered forward and began to leave the trestle. Tom couldn't look down at the river.

He went into the next coach. It was brightly lit, but everyone looked miserable. Carmilla Cain stood in the aisle with her gun. "The kid detective is here," she said into the radio phone. "I'll see you at the junction."

Tom sat down opposite Mr. Nicholson. The principal's long legs filled the space. His eyes were gaunt. "Are you okay, Tom?" he asked, his voice cracking.

"Quiet." Carmilla Cain waved her gun at Mr. Nicholson. "One more word and you're dead meat."

Everyone was silent. All eyes were on Carmilla Cain. She looked out at the bush and snow until Rex's voice crackled from her radio. "*I'm waiting at the junction. I'll stop the train.*"

Carmilla acknowledged his message, then looked around the coach. "I'm leaving, but don't think of causing trouble. It wouldn't be worth the risk."

The train stopped beside a narrow wilderness road. Tom watched as Carmilla Cain got into the waiting pickup truck. Rex waved another signal at the engineer, and the train moved away—the dark woods swallowing the truck. Inside the coach, everyone began talking at once. It wasn't long before the *Prairie Dog Central,* whistle blasting the night, pulled into the station at Muskeg.

* * *

Muskeg was a small town. Most people who gathered at the station, waiting to pick up the children billeted to them, were people of the Cree nation. Tom saw Sadie Cheechov standing on the platform, waving to all the friends she had made on her two week stay in Winnipeg. He was glad to see her.

"Oh, Tom, I can't believe what happened to Mr. Price. Your conductor relayed the news to our station," Sadie said after greeting him. "It will take the police all night to drive here—we're really isolated and the roads are bad this time of year."

"That means the murderers will probably get away."

"Did you actually see what happened at the trestle?" Sadie's eyes were wide.

Tom nodded. "Yes, it was horrible. I'll never forget it." He looked at her dark brown eyes. "Have you noticed anything unusual around here, Sadie? Maybe someone new, in particular a redheaded man with a limp."

She nodded. "He drives a pickup truck with a small camper on the back. Right?"

"Yes!" Tom's eyes glowed. "I can't believe it!"

"Why? Who is he?"

"It's just a hunch. Maybe he's the same man who stopped the train on that trestle, because he lives in the area. He may also be the man who kidnapped Dianne Dorchester. Where have you seen him?"

"A guy from the city has rented a house here for years. He fits your description. Three years ago, he used the house for a while, then disappeared. Then we saw him again about a month ago, when he arrived in town driving the black pickup. Do you really think he's the one who kidnapped Dianne?"

"That house could be a base for kidnapping operations," Tom explained. "There was another girl taken three years ago, in the north. The man that fits your description is called Rex. Does he park the truck at the house?"

Sadie nodded. "In his garage, never in the street. I can show you."

"Great!"

"Want to tell your principal where we're going?"

"I better not—he'll never let me go. But I do have an idea." Tom went to Dietmar Oban. "I need your help."

"Forget it, Austen, not a chance. I can read your mind, and there's no way I'm going into that wilderness in search of murderers or kidnappers. Even if you give me a leather-bound collection of love poems in calligraphy for Charity or tell the whole world you wrote the poems for me."

"Relax, Oban. Just wait ten minutes, then tell Mr. Nicholson I'll be back soon and everything's okay."

"Give it up, Austen. You'll never find them."

"Maybe not, but I'm going to try."

Tom hurried with Sadie through the quiet streets to a lonely house outside town. The black sky was brilliant with stars, and the cold air stung his skin. A chained dog roamed the snow outside the house. "I'm not going in there," Tom said. "Are you sure it'll take the police all night to drive here?"

Sadie nodded. "But look, Tom. There are fresh ski tracks in the snow here. That reminds me, a few days ago, I was tracking south of here with a friend who has a dog team. We saw that man Rex skiing down the river."

"That's really important!" Tom looked at the house.

"This place looks deserted. There aren't any lights."

"But someone's been here tonight," Sadie said. "They may have switched to skis, and headed for the river. I think the pickup truck is inside the garage."

"Why?"

"See the droplets falling from the garage roof? The warmth of the truck is melting the snow."

"You're right," Tom said. "You've got sharp vision."

"Come on," Sadie said. "Let's get some snowshoes. I'll take you to the river where we saw that man."

"Got any skis?"

"Sure, but snowshoes are better. That guy travels on the river. Sometimes creeks and rivers aren't as frozen as they look, and water sticks to the bottom of skis. They slide heavily. We don't want that happening to us, so we'll travel on snowshoes *beside* the river."

Tom and Sadie hurried to her house. "You can meet my parents later, they're visiting my grandmother right now." Sadie lifted snowshoes down from the outside wall and handed Tom some food. "Beef jerky and a Power Bar. I've got more."

They moved away from the house into the nearby bush. Evergreens sagged under the weight of recent snow. The icy air filled Tom's lungs, making them ache. Fortunately, he'd used snowshoes before, because Sadie moved fast. Watching the stars, she led Tom into the wilderness. The sky radiated beautiful colours.

"They're like a massive laser show," Tom exclaimed. "Look how the colours dance up from the horizon toward the stars!"

"The Northern Lights," Sadie said proudly.

Before long, they were looking at the valley of a wandering river. It was white with snow. "This is where I saw that man you call Rex," Sadie said. "He was skiing south."

"What's down there?"

"Not much, except for a few abandoned cabins. People used to come here searching for gold." Sadie smiled. "They never found any. Instead of a mine, we've got all this beauty."

She pointed into the trees. "Someone skied through here recently. See those pine needles and twigs scattered on the snow? Someone brushed past the branches on the way to the river."

"I bet it was Rex and Carmilla Cain. Could they be heading for one of those abandoned cabins?"

Sadie nodded. "River country would be a good place to hide a hostage. Hardly anyone's out there in winter."

"Let's go see."

"We'll stay in wooded areas to keep warm," Sadie said, as they continued their journey. "Out on the river the windchill is bad. Rex probably skis along the river because he's from the city. He'd be afraid of animals in the woods."

"Should we be worried, too?"

Sadie's brown eyes crinkled when she smiled. "Trust me, Tom."

He laughed. "I've said that before, to Dietmar. My only regret is that he's not with us tonight, enjoying himself."

"Look." Ahead was the low shape of a small island surrounded by the snow-covered river. They saw several log cabins. "Somebody's in one of them," Sadie said. "There's smoke drifting from the chimney."

"I can hardly see the cabin, let alone smoke," Tom said. "Where'd you get your eyesight?"

Sadie smiled. "Let's move closer."

Cautiously, they continued down the river. Tom now saw smoke rising above the log cabin. A ladder beside the door led to the snow-covered roof. They also saw two snowmobiles. A path led to a small shed, where smoke drifted into the night from a stovepipe.

"I wonder if Dianne's in there," Tom whispered to Sadie.

She studied the island. "We'll circle around, and approach the cabin through those trees."

Soon, they were sheltered in the woods. Tom studied the windows. A warm light glowed on the closed curtains.

"I'm going to do some snooping," Tom said. "Will you keep watch here?"

Sadie nodded. "Be careful, Tom."

"No problem," he said, wishing it were true.

* * *

Tom followed a path toward the cabin's back door. All around, the snow glistened under the stars. Beside the back door, a curtain billowed gently at a small opening in the window, allowing Tom to see Rex and Carmilla Cain inside. Yellow light from a kerosene lamp glowed against the log walls and old furniture.

Rex was smoking a cigarette in front of a stove. Nearby, Carmilla Cain was in the kitchen area spooning soup into a bowl. When she had finished, she pulled on a ski mask and her parka and headed out the door.

Hiding in the shadows of the cabin, Tom followed the woman as she made her way to the shed. She opened the padlock, hung it on the hasp and went inside.

Dianne was there!

Tom clearly saw her sitting in a wooden chair, before Carmilla Cain closed the door. Tom's heart was pounding. He had to do something!

A short time later, the woman came out of the shed, locked the door and returned to the cabin. Tom followed her back, and peered through the window. He watched as Rex and Carmilla dished out some soup and took their bowls to a big table in the corner. The dim light showed a bookcase nearby. The shelves were bare, except for a gun.

Rex gobbled down his soup, then lit a cigarette.

"Once we cross the border into the States, we'll let the police know where to find the Dorchester kid." He grinned. "They won't be able to search for Price's body until the spring break-up. The ice is too treacherous now for the machinery the cops would need. In spring, there's no guarantee of finding a body. They probably won't even try."

"Operation Golden Child has been too complicated," Carmilla Cain whined. "Now you tell me we're leaving Canada! The Flin Flon kidnapping was much easier. We just carried on with life."

"Sure, but this job has been a lot messier—the girl knows one of us. He's finished, unless he becomes a new person in another country. And *we* have to clear out for a while until things cool down."

"I guess you're right . . . I admit, you did disguise him well. You'd never know he used to be . . ."

"Shut up," Rex barked. "Never, never say his old name. I've told you that. He has a new identity. His name is Albert Booker."

A man came out of a bedroom. He was tall. The yellow lamplight glowed on his bald head. He wore sunglasses and carried a white cane. Tom studied the pointed beard on his chin, and his large nose. He didn't recognize this man at all.

Albert Booker helped himself to some soup and ate in silence.

"What's the matter?" Rex sneered at Booker. "Still sulking because you don't like your disguise? You'll like it plenty when you realize it'll buy your freedom and make you a rich man."

"Hmph," Booker grunted.

"I still say we terminate the girl—she could identify us." Carmilla Cain pulled on her mask. "Time to get the little brat's bowl and spoon."

Carmilla Cain walked under the stars toward the shed. The moment she went inside, Tom raced along the path. Grabbing the padlock, he slapped it into place. There was a muffled shout from Carmilla Cain, then the door shook. But she was trapped.

"One down," Tom said, running toward the cabin. "Two to go."

He cautiously looked in the window. The men sat facing the stove. Rex was reading a magazine and Albert Booker was still eating. Tom carefully opened the door, and began tiptoeing toward the bookcase. He moved slowly, afraid the floor would creak.

Tom reached the bookcase. Holding his breath, he picked up the gun. It was plastic. In a mirror on the wall, he saw the reflection of Rex's face. The man was grinning. His teeth were stained yellow with nicotine.

"I heard the door open," he said. "You're some detective, kid, but not perfect." He held up a gun. "This is a revolver, and it's real. Notice the chamber and its bullets. What you're holding is a pistol, and it's plastic." His smile was nasty as he pointed the revolver straight at Tom. "That's the end of your training as a detective." His finger tightened on the trigger.

Albert Booker slashed Rex's hand with the white cane. Rex hollered in pain and dropped the revolver. Just as quickly, Booker seized it from the floor, and spoke in a gruff voice. "Nobody harms that boy!" He turned to Tom. "You're nothing but trouble. How did you find us?"

"Shoot him," Rex urged.

"No way."

A faint noise sounded on the roof. The men were too busy arguing to notice. Tom stared at the revolver, wondering if somehow he could capture it from Albert Booker.

The man looked at his watch. "Where's Carmilla? She's not back from the shed."

"Maybe . . ." Rex coughed. "Hey, there's smoke coming into the cabin. What's wrong with the stove?" He kneeled beside it. Thick smoke was billowing out. "Something's blocked the stovepipe. I'll climb to the roof and check it." He took a rifle from the wall. "I'd better take this, just in case."

"Don't even think of shooting Tom."

"Relax!" Rex gave Albert Booker a dirty look.

"You're not supposed to know the kid's name."

Booker was silent, as Tom stared at him. *Who is this man? How does he know my name?*

Rex shook his head. "I'm surrounded by fools." He went out the front door into the snow.

Suddenly, there was a twang of sound and a yelp of surprise. Tom ran to the door, just in time to see that a rope had seized Rex's leg, and flipped him upside down. The rifle fell from his hand, and landed in the snow.

"What the . . . ?" Albert Booker ran to the door. "That's a snare! What's going on?"

Rex was hanging from a tree. "Get me down!" he hollered.

Albert Booker quickly pulled on his parka and hurried outside. Then a shape flew off the roof and knocked the tall man into the snow. It was Sadie!

"Tom," she cried, struggling to control Albert Booker. "Grab the rifle!"

"It fell into the snow somewhere! I can't find it!"

Booker broke free of Sadie and ran toward one of the snowmobiles. Leaping on board, he gunned the engine. Within moments, the Ski-Doo was gone, carrying Albert Booker into the night.

* * *

"Rats!" Sadie said, "We almost had him!"

Rex was still yelling, but they just ignored him.

"You blocked the stove pipe," Tom said, as they searched for the rifle. "How?"

"With some branches," Sadie replied.

"And you set the snare?"

She nodded. "I found some rope. My dad taught me that trick."

"What'll we do now?" Tom asked. "Albert Booker is escaping!"

"We can follow the tracks of his Ski-Doo," Sadie replied. "But first, let's secure the prisoners and free Dianne."

"Hey," Tom said, as his hand touched cold metal. "I've found the rifle."

The pair hurried to the shed. Sadie pounded on the door with the rifle butt. "We've got a gun," she cried. "Surrender, and set Dianne free!"

"Don't make me laugh," Carmilla shouted from inside the shed. "You don't know how to use a gun."

Sadie pointed the rifle at a nearby tree and pulled the trigger. The night was shattered by the roar of sound, and snow fell from the tree.

"Quick, Tom," Sadie said. "Open the door, and stand back."

Tom lifted off the padlock and threw open the door. Dianne still sat in the chair. Her face was pale, but her eyes brightened when she saw her friends. Carmilla cringed in a corner.

"You crazy kid," she cried to Sadie. "That rifle's dangerous! Put it down, before someone gets hurt."

"No way, lady." Sadie looked at Dianne. "Can you walk?"

"Yes," Dianne replied. Slowly, she stood up. "I feel stiff, but I'll be okay."

Tom hurried into the shed. "Dianne, I'm so glad you're safe."

She hugged him. "I can't believe you've rescued me, Tom. Thank you!"

He grinned, feeling proud and happy. "It's all because of Sadie."

Dianne hugged Sadie. "I've dreamed of this moment, ever since they kidnapped me. It's been so lonely up here."

"You're safe now," Sadie said.

Before long, both Carmilla Cain and Rex were tied with ropes, and padlocked inside the shed. Tom and Sadie stood in the snow beside Dianne, who was wearing a parka and toque and double layers of gloves; she shivered as Sadie started the snowmobile.

"Maybe that Ski-Doo's too small for three," Dianne said.

"We're not leaving anyone behind," Sadie said, cranking the accelerator. The Ski-Doo roared. "Climb on board."

The wind stung their faces as the Ski-Doo raced north along the river. Sadie pointed at the tracks left by Albert Booker's machine. "He's having trouble steering it," she cried. "We'll catch up fast."

The brilliant colours of the Northern Lights still danced through the night. The river was pale beneath the sky; all around were dark hills and trees. Tom and Dianne leaned toward Sadie, trying to stay warm behind the windshield. Tom's fingertips were numb.

Engine roaring, they cut suddenly toward the woods. "He's making for town," Sadie called. "See the lights glowing ahead?"

"Why would he go there?"

"He's panicked," Sadie replied. "He's not thinking straight. He's just desperate to escape."

The lights of Muskeg came closer. Then Sadie pointed. "Look!"

Ahead was the bobbing red light of Albert Booker's Ski-Doo. He had reached the main street of town and was now heading toward the railway station, where the *Prairie Dog Central* waited.

Sadie stopped at her house and they all jumped off the Ski-Doo. "I'll get Dianne inside—that was a cold trip up the river, and she was in the shed a long time. I'll also tell my parents what's happening so they can get help."

"I'll see where Albert Booker's gone," Tom said. He walked quickly along the street; his watch said three in the morning. The railway station was deserted and dark, and something howled, far off in the night. Tom walked slowly onto the platform—he was afraid. The train loomed above. Where was Albert Booker?

"Looking for me?" a voice whispered. "I need a hostage. Turn around."

Albert Booker stood in the shadows, holding the revolver. His false beard was peeling off and he'd lost his sunglasses. He pulled a rubber nose away from his face. He was no longer Albert Booker.

"But . . ." Tom stammered. "But . . . you're Mr. Price!"

9

The teacher's eyes stared at Tom. "I like you, Tom, but you've ruined everything." He looked at the locomotive. "We're leaving town, you and me, right now."

"Stop this, Mr. Price. Give yourself up."

"Quiet!" The man leveled the gun at Tom. "Do exactly as I tell you. I don't want to use this."

They climbed the steel ladder into the locomotive cab. "The steam's up," Mr. Price said, studying a gauge. He released the brakes. "So far, nothing to it. The engineer was a good teacher."

The locomotive thudded, straining at the weight of the coaches. Slowly, the train gathered speed. Tom heard a cry. Sadie and her father had just reached the station on their Ski-Doo. They watched in amazement as the train moved down the track and into the night.

A cold wind swept through the open window, but the fire gave warmth. Neither of them spoke as the train thundered through the night. The big headlight lit up the tracks, rocks and snow. Tom saw the trestle ahead where Mr. Price's death had been faked.

Suddenly, Mr. Price grabbed the brake. "Hang tight," he yelled as the steel wheels screeched against the tracks. "We're stopping!"

The *Prairie Dog Central* came to a screaming halt in the middle of the trestle. Up ahead, Tom saw the tracks blocked by a barricade of Ski-Doos. He recognized the people—they were from Muskeg. Sadie and her father were with them.

Mr. Price leaned out the window. "They've blocked both ends of the trestle with Ski-Doos." Sweat poured down his face. The gun trembled in his hand. "I'm not going to prison," he said desperately. "I couldn't take living in a cell." He waved the gun at Tom. "It's your fault!"

"Give yourself up, Mr. Price."

"Never!" He pointed at the steel ladder. "Climb down to the trestle. You're still my hostage."

Tom stepped onto the ladder. Steam seeped from the train, and a cold wind blew past. Mr. Price followed Tom down to the trestle. Sadie and the others were walking toward them.

Mr. Price fired the revolver into the air. The blast of sound echoed down the valley. The people kept coming along the trestle.

"I'll shoot," Mr. Price screamed. "Don't come any closer!"

"You'll get twenty-five years for murder if you shoot

anyone," Tom said urgently. "That's a quarter century behind bars, Mr. Price. Don't do it!"

The gun fired again. The people kept coming forward.

"You're going to prison, Mr. Price. *Give up*."

Mr. Price pulled the trigger again, but the gun was empty. With a cry of grief, he threw it from the trestle. "I'm not going to prison. My life would be over."

Tom looked at the group of people, and started to edge in their direction. Suddenly, Mr. Price grabbed him by the throat. "Back off," he screamed at the people. "Don't risk this boy's life. Let me through."

Sadie and the others let Mr. Price through. He walked cautiously to the end of the trestle, fiercely gripping Tom's neck. "Just cooperate, Tom, and we'll get out of this faster."

Tom could hardly draw breath into his lungs.

Then Sadie spoke. "My Ski-Doo's fast," she said, pointing at it under some nearby trees. "I'll give you the keys, if you give us Tom. We promise not to follow."

Mr. Price snatched the keys from her hand as she came forward. He shoved Tom face-forward into the snow, and hurried to the Ski-Doo.

Suddenly, there was a *twang*, and Mr Price flew into the air. He was hanging upside down by one foot, his face ashen white.

Sadie had a huge smile on her face. "The snare strikes again," she beamed. "Are you okay, Tom?"

He hugged her. "You bet, Sadie. Thanks for everything!"

Sadie hugged him back. "You're welcome, Tom. Any time."

* * *

Duncan leaned back in his chair. "Wow!" He wiped sweat from his forehead. "I was really worried when Mr. Price had that gun on the trestle. Someone could have been killed."

Tom nodded. "He'd have done almost anything to avoid prison. But now he's behind bars."

Duncan's beagle pup, Frisky, bounded into the room. He dashed between the boys, demanding affection.

"Sadie was so brave," Duncan said. "Have you seen her since then?"

"Sure," Tom replied. "We're good friends."

"I guess you ended up in Mr. Stones' class?"

Tom nodded. "He was my teacher when Dianne got kidnapped again."

"Imagine that happening twice," Duncan said. "Her name should be in the book of world records."

Tom took a game of Clue down from the shelf. "This time, I'm going to win." He chose to be Professor Plum, and Duncan selected Colonel Mustard. They set up the pieces on the board, shuffled the cards and began playing. "Tom," Duncan said, "whatever happened to you and Dianne? I think secretly she liked you."

"Our class had a second Valentine's Day when Dianne came back. Remember the card she was making at her desk? She gave it to me."

"Excellent."

"Dietmar made up a poem for Charity and gave it to her inside a Valentine's card." Tom shook his head. "She liked it better than my poetry!"

Duncan gave his cousin an affectionate smile. He

moved Colonel Mustard into the dining room and collected his first evidence. "So, what happened to Donald and Walt?"

Tom rolled a one. "Terrific," he muttered, watching in dismay as Duncan moved swiftly to the lounge. "Mr. Dorchester put up the money for Donald to try the medicine in the States, but it didn't work. Then a researcher at the University of Manitoba found a real cure, and now Donald's fine."

"Great! But what about Walt? Why'd he run from the station if he was innocent?"

Tom continued moving Professor Plum toward the library. "He just panicked under the pressure. After life returned to normal, Walt made up with his wife and the family was back together. Remember how Walt was in St. Boniface during the ice festival? He'd been visiting his wife, hoping to patch things up."

Duncan used the secret passage to reach the conservatory, where he obtained more evidence. "I guess Carmilla Cain posed as a reporter," he said, "so she could accuse Walt of being a kidnapper. His arrest would have given the gang enough time to escape from Canada. But I don't understand why Walt had a counterfeit bill. He used it to buy coffee, remember?"

Tom nodded. He managed to get Professor Plum into the library, where he collected his first evidence.

"Mr. Price slipped the bill into Walt's pocket during the bus ride to the station."

"I should have guessed that," Duncan said. He rolled a six, which took Colonel Mustard straight into the billiard room. There was a happy smile on Duncan's face as he recorded more information on his notepad.

"Help me out," Tom whispered to the die. He rolled a six, which took him into the hall. "Things are looking better! Did you figure out how they faked Mr. Price's death?"

"I think so." Duncan effortlessly took Colonel Mustard into the library. "I'm getting close to making an accusation," he grinned. "There must have been a fake body inside Carmilla's rucksack. Did they dress it in Mr. Price's parka and ski pants, then throw it off the train?"

"That's right," Tom said. He moved the professor toward the dining room. "The dummy was weighted to fall through the ice. Rex planned to retrieve it later, just in case anyone looked for a body. Mr. Price hid in the washroom until the train reached the junction, then slipped out of the empty coach and waited in the bush. When the train was gone, he joined Rex and Carmilla in the pickup truck."

"Why did Mr. Price frame Walt?" Duncan asked. "So he wouldn't be suspected himself?"

For a moment, Tom didn't reply. He was watching Duncan move Colonel Mustard toward the study. He was probably planning to follow the secret passage to the kitchen, then announce his solution. He had to be stopped! "Mr. Price saw me interviewed on television. He heard my theory about Rex maybe working with someone from Queenston School and decided to make me suspect Walt."

"Because of Walt's criminal past?"

"That's right," Tom replied. His only hope was to reach the dining room on his next move. "Mr. Price deliberately gave me the assignment to research drunk

driving. He knew I'd find the article about Walt going
to prison. Then he hid my cryptogram book in Walt's
boiler room, and sent me in search of a broom and
dust pan so I'd find the fake code."

"Walt looked pretty guilty when he didn't have an
alibi for the morning the ransom was paid."

Tom nodded. "I guess that's exactly what Mr. Price
hoped for when he phoned Bryan Newgass and tipped
him off that Walt was in Chinatown with our class. He
was sure the reporter would grill Walt about his prison
record."

"After the ceremony at the Legislative Building, did
Mr. Price call Rex's cellular phone?"

"That's right. Rex needed to know that Mr. Dorchester
was on his way to the bookstore with the ransom."

"Mr. Price made a slip," Duncan said. "He shouldn't
have known the secret police information that the second vehicle was a van. He also lived in River Heights,
where some of the ransom money was spent in stores."
Duncan rolled a one, giving Tom his chance.

Tom whispered a prayer, then rolled. "I've done it!"
Joyfully, he took Professor Plum into the dining room.
"I'm prepared to make my accusation!"

Duncan shook his head, unhappily. "Before you do,
tell me about Mr. Nicholson. Why was he given all that
money in Chinatown?"

"He was part of a group that held a winning lottery
ticket. Mr. Nicholson was collecting his share."

"He was never part of the kidnappers' gang?"

Tom shook his head. "Now, at last, my moment of
victory. Open the envelope, please."

Duncan took out the cards that held the solution.

Tom consulted his notepad. "I accuse Miss Scarlett."

Duncan laid a card on the board. Miss Scarlett stared at them with sinister eyes.

"I knew it," Tom cried with delight. "And she used the knife."

Duncan turned over the knife card.

"Yes!" Tom punched the air with his fist. "Finally, I've beaten you at this game!"

"Where did the crime take place?" Duncan asked.

"In the dining room, of course."

Duncan laid the final card on the board. It showed the library.

"But . . ." Tom stared in dismay at the card. "But you went into the dining room collecting evidence. I thought . . ."

"I faked you out." Duncan's grin was ear-to-ear. "I guess that means I'm the winner . . . and a pretty good detective, too. Anyway, Tom, thanks for a great time. Let's do it again, soon."

Eric Wilson

When Eric Wilson was young he attended Queenston School in Winnipeg and blushed whenever girls glanced his way. Wanting to be the third Hardy Boy, Eric dreamed up detective stories while serving on his school's crossing patrol at the corner of Kingsway and Waterloo. Eventually he became a teacher who wrote for his students; now his adventure stories are shared by kids in many places. "I hope this shows," says Eric, "that people who feel kind of ordinary, as I did, can still see their dreams come true."

COLD MIDNIGHT IN VIEUX QUÉBEC

A Tom Austen Mystery

ERIC WILSON

Tom crouched lower as he raced toward the darkness ahead. Then he suddenly straightened up and yelled. He was heading straight for the cliff.

The leaders of the world's superpowers have agreed to meet in Quebec City to put an end to chemical weapons— but powerful forces will stop at nothing to prevent the agreement from being signed. From the first chilling page, you will be gripped by suspense as you follow Tom Austen and Dietmar Oban through the ancient, mysterious streets of Vieux Québec in quest of world peace.

"It was excellent. The ending was very romantic."
—*Laura T., Charlottetown, Prince Edward Island*

CODE RED AT THE SUPERMALL

A Tom and Liz Austen Mystery

ERIC WILSON

They swam past gently moving strands of seaweed and pieces of jagged coral, then Tom almost choked in horror. A shark was coming straight at him, ready to strike.

Have you ever visited a shopping mall that has sharks and piranhas, a triple-loop rollercoaster, 22 waterslides, an Ice Palace, submarines, 828 stores, and a major mystery to solve? Soon after Tom and Liz Austen arrive at the West Edmonton Mall a bomber strikes and they must follow a trail that leads through the fabled splendours of the supermall . . . to hidden danger.

"I really like the part when Liz stood up for her rights toward Chad. That's how every girl or woman should be."
—*Suzanne M., Calgary, Alberta*

"I'm from Pakistan and I don't like people calling me names so I'm glad Eric Wilson wrote about racism."
—*Atif B., Hamilton, Ontario*

THE GREEN GABLES DETECTIVES

A Liz Austen Mystery

ERIC WILSON

I almost expected to see Anne signalling to Diana from her bedroom window as we climbed the slope toward Green Gables, then Makiko grabbed my arm. "Danger!"

While visiting the famous farmhouse known as Green Gables, Liz Austen and her friends are swept up in baffling events that lead them from an ancient cemetery to a haunted church, and to then a heart-stopping showdown in a deserted lighthouse as fog swirls across Prince Edward Island. Be prepared for eerie events and unbearable suspense as you join the Green Gables Detectives for a thrilling adventure.

"I did a project on *The Green Gables Detectives* and got 95%. My favourite part was when Liz swallowed the oyster."
—*Paul H., Fortune, Newfoundland*

SPIRIT IN THE RAINFOREST

A Tom and Liz Austen Mystery

ERIC WILSON

The branches trembled, then something slipped away into the darkness of the forest. "That was Mosquito Joe!" Tom exclaimed.

"Or his spirit," Liz said. "Let's get out of here."

The rainforest of British Columbia holds many secrets, but none stranger than those of Nearby Island. After hair-raising events during a Pacific storm, Tom and Liz Austen seek answers among the island's looming trees. Alarmed by the ghostly shape of the hermit Mosquito Joe, they look for shelter in a deserted school in the rainforest. Then, in the night, Tom and Liz hear a girl's voice crying, *"Beware! Beware!"*

"My family was surprised I was reading, but I love this book. It was inspiring and interesting, and I highly recommend that other kids read it."

—*Krystle T., LeFory, Ontario*

VAMPIRES OF OTTAWA

A Liz Austen Mystery

ERIC WILSON

Suddenly the vampire rose up from behind a tombstone and fled, looking like an enormous bat with his black cape streaming behind in the moonlight.

Within the walls of a gloomy estate known as Blackwater, Liz Austen discovers the strange world of Baron Nicolai Zaba, a man who lives in constant fear. What is the secret of the ancient chapel's underground vault? Why are the words *In Evil Memory* scrawled on a wall? Who secretly threatens the Baron? All the answers lie within these pages but be warned: *reading this book will make your blood run cold.*

"I enjoyed *Vampires of Ottawa* a lot. Eric Wilson really had my mind going a couple of times!"
—*Alyson B., Perth Andover, New Brunswick*

THE KOOTENAY KIDNAPPER

A Tom Austen Mystery

ERIC WILSON

Silence came to the cave, broken only by the drip of water on rock. Cold and loneliness spread through Tom's tired body. Suddenly, Tattoo's hand lashed out.

What is the secret lurking in the ruins of a lonely ghost town in the mountains of British Columbia? Solving this mystery is only one of the challenges facing Tom Austen after he arrives in B.C. with his sidekick, Dietmar Oban, and learns that a young girl has disappeared without a trace. Then a boy is kidnapped, and electrifying events quickly carry Tom to a breathtaking climax deep underground in Cody Caves, where it is forever night . . .

"I didn't enjoy reading until my mom and dad gave me *The Kootenay Kidnapper.* It just lifted me off my feet."
—*Brian F., Sooke, British Columbia*